Praise for
Mercè Rodoreda

"Rodoreda plumbs a sadness that reaches beyond historic circumstances . . . an almost voluptuous vulnerability."

—Natasha Wimmer, *The Nation*

"Rodoreda had bedazzled me by the sensuality with which she reveals things within the atmosphere of her novels."

—Gabriel García Márquez

"It is a total mystery to me why [Rodoreda] isn't widely worshipped. . . . She's on my list of authors whose works I intend to have read all of before I die. Tremendous, tremendous writer."

—John Darnielle, The Mountain Goats

"When you read [*Death in Spring*], read it for its beauty, for the way it will surprise and subvert your desires, and as a testament to the human spirit in the face of brutality and willful inhumanity."

—Jesmyn Ward, NPR

"The humor in the stories, as well as their thrill of realism, comes from a Nabokovian precision of observation and transformation of plain experience into enchanting prose."

—*Los Angeles Times*

Also by
Mercè Rodoreda

A Broken Mirror
Camellia Street
Death in Spring
My Christina and Other Stories
The Selected Stories of Mercè Rodoreda
The Time of the Doves

WAR, SO MUCH WAR

MERCÈ RODOREDA

Translated from
the Catalan by
Maruxa Relaño &
Martha Tennent

OPEN LETTER
LITERARY TRANSLATIONS FROM THE UNIVERSITY OF ROCHESTER

First edition, 2015

Library of Congress Cataloging-in-Publication Data:

Rodoreda, Mercè, 1908-1983.
[Quanta, quanta guerra. English]
War, so much war / by Mercè Rodoreda ; translated from the Catalan by
Maruxa Relaño & Martha Tennent. — First edition.
pages cm
ISBN 978-1-940953-22-9 (pbk. : alk. paper) — ISBN 1-940953-22-7 (pbk. : alk. paper)
I. Relaño, Maruxa, translator. II. Tennant, Martha, translator. III. Title.
PC3941.R57Q3613 2015
849'.9352—dc23
2015013345

This project is supported in part by an award from the National Endowment for the Arts.

ART WORKS.
arts.gov

Translation of this novel was made possible thanks to the support of the Ramon Llull Institut.

LLLL institut
ramon llull
Catalan Language and Culture

Printed on acid-free paper in the United States of America.

Text set in Fournier, a typeface designed by Pierre Simon Fournier (1712–1768),
a French punch-cutter, typefounder, and typographic theoretician.

Design by N. J. Furl

Open Letter is the University of Rochester's nonprofit, literary translation press:
Lattimore Hall 411, Box 270082, Rochester, NY 14627

www.openletterbooks.org

"The sleep of reason produces monsters."
—Francisco de Goya

"What makes me take this trip to Africa?
There is no explanation."
—Saul Bellow

"A great ravel of flights from nothing to nothing."
—D. H. Lawrence

WAR, SO MUCH WAR

PART ONE

I

MIDNIGHT

I WAS BORN AT MIDNIGHT, IN THE AUTUMN OF THE YEAR, WITH A
birthmark on my forehead no bigger than a lentil. When I made
my mother angry, she would stand with her back to me and say,
you remind me of Cain. Josep had a scar in the shape of a fish
on his left thigh, on the inside; it was funny. Rossend, the son of
the junkman who lent us his donkey and wagon to take our carnations to market, had a red-tipped nose that was funny. Ramon, the
butcher's son, had pointy ears that were funny. I wasn't funny. If
they ever teamed up against me to taunt me for not wanting to join
in their games, I drove them back by shouting that the Devil was
my uncle and he had marked me on the forehead before I was born
so he could find me easily, even in the middle of a group of boys. I
was as blond as a gold thread. When I was three, everyone mistook
me for a girl because Mother had never cut my hair and it fell in
ringlets down the sides of my neck. The day Mother took me to
see Father Sebastià to have me admitted to school, Father Sebastià
gave me a sad look and said: We don't accept girls. Mother lapsed
into all manner of explanations. It pained her to cut such beautiful
hair; I was too little and would be cold with my hair all chopped
off. And while she was explaining, I, who already knew how to
write my name, strode to the blackboard, and grasping a piece of
chalk, white on black, scribbled in large, crooked letters: Adrià

Guinart. Father Sebastià noticed at once and, clasping his hands together, exclaimed, "A veritable archangel!"

I started school with my hair cropped, distressed by the change but wiser than the other boys. Father Sebastià had me sit beside him when he taught Sacred History; my gaze troubled him if I sat on the bench: too much like an owl, he said. We had a thick folder full of large holy pictures that was kept locked in the cupboard where we stored notebooks, pencils, and chalk. While he spoke, I—it was always I—was supposed to wield a wooden stick to point to the things he mentioned: the Dead Sea, the Staff of Moses, the Tables of the Law, the Tree of the Knowledge of Good and Evil, Adam and Eve wearing fig leaves. Now point to Solomon. I was always mortified when I had to point to the fellow who lost his strength when they cut his hair. Point to the herald angel. Blond, with ringlets like I had before starting school, the blooming lily in his hand, and feathery wings—a blue stripe, a red stripe—the angel hovered in mid-air before Mary. When it was time for the image of the Great Flood, all the boys in the class, even the sleepiest, most distracted, perked up. As I followed the arching rainbow of colors with the pointer, I could feel myself floating between the green and the purple, the yellow and the pink . . . Hadn't Father Sebastià called me an archangel? Archangels flew. Cain and Abel. I held my breath. Abel was grazing his sheep. Cain was sweating and plowing. I was dreaming Sacred History, dreaming angels, dreaming saints, dreaming of myself living Sacred History, crossing deserts and making water flow from springs. On the days when the Crucifixion print was shown, as soon as I reached the field of carnations, I would race from one end to the other, and stand on tiptoes, reaching up as far as I could to hear the stars whispering, poor thing, poor thing, he doesn't have wings . . .

The house was ancient, the sink had a terrible stench, the faucet leaked. On windy days the cold crept in through the cracks, but in good weather the smell of flowers permeated every corner. On the Sundays when my father wasn't of a mind to visit his cousins, he would take me for a walk. We spent hours sitting by the side of the road, and sometimes the air winnowed threads from the hearts of stunted flowers, and some would catch in my clothes. It seemed to me that people were all the same: with legs, with thighs, with eyes, mouths, teeth. I walked along, straight as a ninepin, holding the hand of my father who was tall and very good. I don't know why I resented girls; if I ever got my hands on one, I would wring her neck like you would a bird's. They exhaust motherly love.

A neighbor who worked in the textile factory had a daughter. One Saturday afternoon she asked my mother to keep the baby. I was anxious: Mother had announced that she had gone to buy me a sister and I would never again be alone; we would have a little girl at home who would laugh and cry. When I asked her why she had bought a girl and not a boy, she simply stated that she had received notice that it would be a girl. That Saturday afternoon my mother said she had to go see somebody about selling the carnations; she told me to keep an eye on the neighbor's baby and to be especially careful not to let the cat near her. When Mother left, I went to peep at the sleeping baby and at the cat, which she had shut in the kitchen. The baby's name was Mariona; she was pink and had gold earrings. She was lying across two chairs that had been pushed together. I picked her up and put her on the floor. The moan she made took my breath away. I started undressing her the way you would a doll: off with the bodice, off with the panties, off with the swaddling clothes, off with the woolen slippers. I couldn't remove her earrings because I didn't know how to unfasten them. When I had her naked as a little worm, I placed her on a towel and, tugging on it, I dragged her to the edge of the field. She was half awake, and the sunlight roused her completely. I curled up beside her and studied her bare gums and her hair—just a few hairs, and very fine. Her eyes were the color of violets, dappled with gold. Intoxicated by the thrill of feeling so old beside she who was so small, I stood up and went to pluck all the violets. Her eyes would be the only violets. In the middle of the field, between two rows of carnations, above the irrigation ditch, I fashioned for her a bed of round, green violet leaves. I carried her there, fearing I might break her, and put her down. She stopped breathing for a moment, and then, all at once, with her mouth wide open, the crying began. I had the urge to take her up to the roof terrace, where the railing was broken, and throw her down. I ran to fetch the cat. I put it down next to her and it sat very still. Look at the cat . . . look . . . I made her little hand stroke the cat's back, but suddenly it wanted loose and jumped on her and scratched her chest. My mother once told someone—I don't remember who—that when children are left to cry for too long they break. Be still, little girl. I was afraid she might shatter the way a cup does when you drop it. The little girl was covered in blood. Mother whacked me. I wanted to die. I climbed onto the roof of the toolshed and threw myself down. I fell on all fours. I spent all that night, that moonlit night, hurling myself from the shed to the ground. Shortly thereafter, my first little sister was born. And on that night I planted myself. When I had dug a deep hole at the foot of the hazel tree, I climbed in and covered myself with dirt up to my knees. I had taken the watering can with me, and I watered myself. I wanted to grow roots, I wanted to be all branches and leaves.

—

Mother was from the neighborhood of Sarrià in Barcelona, and she had a field of carnations between Sarrià and Sant Gervasi, near the train line to Sabadell. I helped in the tasks of watering, taking cuttings, and picking flowers. We worked from sunup to sundown. My father died when I was eleven. He was a train driver. He had a mustache and large, tranquil eyes. When I was little, to get me to sleep he would sit me on his lap and sing me the song about the wheels that go round and round, round and round. He said there was a fiery moon the first time the man appeared on the tracks. A thick fog lay asleep above the trees to the right. And a man was walking right down the middle of the tracks toward the train. As soon as my father saw him, he blew the whistle. The man, who was small at first but started getting bigger, walked on as though there were no train bearing down on him. He got so close my father could see the clothes he was wearing: light-colored trousers and a yellow-and-black striped shirt. My father braked. There was screaming in the compartments. My father got off the train, followed by a group of passengers. They found no one on the tracks. Father had to give the company an account of what had happened to explain why the train was late. Everything would have ended with that if a year later, in the same spot but on a pitch-black night with snowflakes falling calmly from the sky, the man walking along the tracks had not appeared again, in the same attire: pale trousers and a yellow and black shirt. The train was moving at full speed, the wheels singing that song about wheels that go round and round. The minute my father spotted him, he blew the whistle several times, but the stubborn man kept getting closer. Until, finally, his heart pounding, my father was forced to brake. Frightened screams came from the passenger cars. My father got off the train. There was no one on the tracks. Together with some passengers, they scoured the surrounding area. Nothing turned up. My father sensed that the people didn't believe him, that they were eyeing him as though he were crazy. Again, he had to notify the company. If they ever came to suspect that the train driver was seeing visions . . . And on a moonlit night, an expanse of silvery fields on either side of the track, the man in pale trousers and striped shirt again appeared in the distance, as he had on the two previous occasions. My father said he closed his eyes . . . and did not brake. And with every one of his senses he felt the sound of bones being crushed. The company did not fire him, but he was moved to another line. He operated a dilapidated old train that was as subdued as a turtle and only made short hauls. Plunged into the well of that mystery, he died of a heart attack shortly thereafter. Mother did not weep for him. The carnations were hard work and we had to carry on. The house began to lose its color, as if everything—kitchen utensils, furniture, and walls—were bathed in a sickly light.

One day I sassed my mother, and the very next day she spoke of my brother for the first time. When I came home wet and dirty from having diverted the irrigation ditches, she would say, without looking at me: I had your brother brush the junkman's donkey. Tomorrow at dawn your brother will help me load the carnations. Your brother . . . But I had no brother. One evening I thought

I saw him hiding in the camellia shed. He looked just like me. I moved closer, there was no one in the camellias.

I started running away at night. I would jump out the kitchen window into the field and squeeze through the parted spikes of the gate to the street. I was suffocating at home. The trains that sped past in the night kept me company. I never left the neighborhood. The locked houses, the dead windows, the balconies with the shadows of hanging flowers, the cool nocturnal water of a fountain in a square, a stone bench at the entrance to a house: They were my companions. The streets with no living soul were my palaces, my joy, my fear. The streets lined with ancient trees, their tall branches on the point of thrusting themselves upon me and sweeping me aloft: They were my nightmares. At daybreak I would return to the prison of my home.

Ever since the war began, Rossend—the junkman's son, two years my senior—had not stopped talking about it. He told me he was joining up. Why don't you come with me?

II

THE ESCAPE

FRESH AIR STREAMED IN THROUGH THE WINDOW. WHEN THE
dining-room clock struck three, I rose and left without even
washing my face and, you might say, with only the clothes on my
back. I had taken some fifty steps when something made me turn
around and glance back at the house. The moonlight fell full on
it. My father stood at the door watching me, holding me—still a
little boy—in his arms. It was the first night that I roamed alone
through streets outside my neighborhood. I ran. Goodbye carnations, *adéu*!

Rossend and I had arranged to meet at the Jardinets de Gràcia.
He was going to show up in a van, but he didn't explain how he
would come by it. I'm friends with a very important captain and
we'll do just as we please. There was no Rossend, no van at the
Jardinets. I couldn't go home again, no matter what happened now.
I had taken it into my head to go off to war and that is what I
would do. Maybe Rossend, who was also running away, hadn't
been able to slip out. I paced back and forth beneath the blue
lampposts for a long time; then I sat on a bench. I got up from the
bench. I sat down again. I crossed the street. I hid in a doorway
because people were approaching. I sat on a stone bench in front
of which were a fountain, plants, trees. The moonlight pierced
through the leaves and dappled the ground with light. I stood and
headed back to the other bench. For a long while, and then longer

still, I wandered from one place to another. Until, finally, a white van with red and black letters smeared across the side stopped in front of me. Rossend and three other fellows jumped out just as the sirens started to wail. Right away flashes from the antiaircraft artillery began to sweep the sky. I would have liked to see a bomb fall. The plane flew low overhead; you could hear its engine just above the houses. The antiaircraft guns spit fire. Run for cover! Everyone, against the wall. Antiaircraft weapons are deadlier than bombs. These sirens . . . Rossend covered his ears and closed his eyes. One of the boys, the one who seemed the youngest of the three, said with a grown-up voice, if these sirens bother you, I'd like to see you at the front where they never stop. I've just come from the front, said another boy, who had a red scarf around his neck and a dagger in his belt, and they can bomb away all they please, it won't get them anywhere. We're stronger. You can't mess around with the will of the people. Them on the other side, when they catch sight of us, they take off running. I swear. They hide. I stand above the trench with the butt of my rifle propped against my thigh . . . So they can take your picture, said the boy with the thick voice. Shut up. Do they shoot to kill? Rossend asked. Shut up. And without looking at us the boy who hadn't uttered a word the whole time said, but you've never even been to the front. Oh, is that so? And this wound on my thigh, what's that supposed to mean? He rolled up one of the legs of his trousers and showed us a red scar at knee level. You got that when some animal kicked you. You always have to contradict me. Because I know you and I know how you like to string lies together . . . The airplane engine rumbled in the distance. The antiaircraft guns were still sweeping the sky. Everyone, in the van! Now we'll start living, Rossend said as he took the wheel. The boy with the red scarf sat beside him.

Me and the others climbed in the back. Half a dozen rifles were stashed in the corner. If I liked the idea of going off to war, it was, among other things, because I would be going with Rossend: I'd known him since I was little, we played together, we were friends, he lived near my house. I didn't know where the others were from, where they were born, who their parents were.

Their presence made me uncomfortable. If at least Rossend had let me sit beside him, but he was ignoring me. The boys stretched out on the floor of the van, and I did the same. They stank. They were breathing heavily. From time to time the guy with the thick voice made a strange sound with his teeth. The jolting of the van lulled me to sleep. Why did Rossend have to be such good friends with that fellow with the red scarf who stood up in the trenches, when the others said he was a liar? Exhaustion muddled my mind, and I saw my father waving goodbye at the foot of a floating house with a facing of bright, gleaming tiles and blue lampposts, and moonlight streaming through the leaves, until everything began to spin: Father, Father's hand, gleaming house, moonlight, blue lampposts, lances of light against the sky. I was asleep when we reached the front.

III

IN THE WOODS

I LOST MY WAY AND DIDN'T KNOW WHICH DIRECTION TO TAKE, until a carriage road jumped out in front of me, so to speak, and I followed it. It was a fine day, a sunny day, an autumn day as I had never seen before in my short life. Sitting with my back against the trunk of a pine tree, I took several deep breaths. The ground was blanketed with pine needles but I couldn't contemplate it calmly: The wound in my arm was tender and the bandage was stained with blood. At the entrance to the carriage road I found some rope, almost new and rather long. I'll keep a piece. I cut it with the penknife my father had given me just before he saw the man walking into the train for the first time. The knife had many different tools: It was a knife, spoon, corkscrew, paper cutter, awl, scissors, and screwdriver. My mother scolded him: It's dangerous, keep it till he's older.

At my feet, a row of ants were dragging a beetle belly up; it was wiggling its feet, with nowhere to latch on to. A pinecone landed on my back. I looked up to see where it had fallen from. A flight of birds crossed the sky. The half-dead beetle that the ants were towing was large, black, shiny. Potbellied. I felt the urge to turn it over on its feet and scatter the ants. A cannon shot dispersed the flock of birds. The ants were still dragging the beetle. A second cannon shot went off farther afield, as if borne by the wind. I was standing, on the point of fleeing, when I spotted a boy behind some trees darting by as though possessed; he didn't seem real. Holding his arm out in front of him, he pointed in the direction of the cannon shot. Before disappearing into the pine trees, he shouted: Go home! For a long, long time I stood there thinking about the boy and what he had said. But I was hungry and hunger distracted me. I crushed the pinecone with a stone; the pine nuts were puny and bitter. I could have eaten a horse. For hours upon hours nothing had entered my stomach except a few clusters of green grapes and water from the river down below. My shoulders hurt from unloading sacks of lentils and potatoes and swinging an axe to chop wood for the soldiers' kitchen. My wound ached. Everything ached.

Rossend and his friends disappeared right away. Juli-Juli, the plumber who washed pots and plates with me in the kitchen, told me they had been taken away during the night to build trenches in some village. And he said to me: What are you doing here, so young? Beat it! If you can.

The entrance to the ant nest was blocked by the beetle's carapace, its legs scarcely moving now, and the ants scurried about like mad trying to find a way to maneuver it inside. I tripped on another piece of rope. The first scrap I had cut was in my pocket. My sole possessions were my father's knife and that bit of rope. A sloping path ran across the carriage way. Standing between the road and the path, I chose the latter because it was narrow, the weeds around it tall. One final cannon shot rang out, even farther away than the second one, and at that moment I heard a man's voice giving orders: Jump, you fool! Jump!

IV

THE HANGED MAN

A LARGE SACK SUSPENDED FROM A TREE WAS SWINGING BACK AND forth, and from it emerged the head of a man with a straight, taut rope behind it. His face was white, his tongue black, his lips purple. By the tree, just beneath the hanged man's feet, was a rock; I climbed on it and cut the rope. The hanged man crashed to the ground and hit his head, frightening me so much that I was sure I had killed him instead of saving him. He was young, with black hair and bushy eyebrows. Just as I was thinking that he had surrendered his soul to God, he opened one eye and immediately closed it again. He hadn't the strength to hold my gaze. After a while he sat up halfway, and I helped him as he struggled to climb out of the sack. He snapped at me angrily, with a husky voice that seemed to come from beyond the grave: Why did you cut the rope?

For a long time—who is to say how long—his breathing was belabored. Give me some water . . . I'm suffocating . . . I rushed down to the river and, using a jar I found in his haversack, brought him some water; I held his head with one hand and poured water down his throat with the other. He coughed with every attempt; the effort was wearing him out, and finally his head dropped to the side. All of a sudden he revived. If I climbed into the sack to hang myself it's because I wanted a shroud covering me when I died, to keep the vultures from picking the flesh off my bones if my body wasn't found in time to be buried. And what about your head? I asked. My head, he said, they can have it. For all the good it's done me . . . He grasped his neck with both hands and tightened his grip. Maybe this way it won't hurt so much. Pour some more water down me. You look hungry. There's some bread in my bag. I can't even swallow my own saliva. My tongue is swollen. Keep me company. He had me lie down beside him and we covered ourselves with the sack. As I lay there, half-asleep, surrounded by sylvan scents, I could hear the dull sound of a far-away conversation. I no longer remembered that I was sleeping next to a life I had saved. I would travel the world, I would help others, I would save lives. The stars above us seemed to be ushering away the night, and yet it would be a long time before morning dawned.

—<

. . . I made this sack out of four sacks I stole from the mill. Lying with his face to the sky, the hanged man spoke as if in a dream. From time to time he turned his head and looked at me. One whole day it took me to undo the seams and resew them in a different shape, using a sack needle, pushing the string through the holes. I made one sack out of the four. I left two sections unsewed so I could stick my arms through, tie the sack to my neck and slip on the rope collar with the slipknot. The hanged man began to weep with sadness; I gave him a good slap on the back to stop his crying and stood up. Don't leave me, don't leave me . . . Just when I was resolved to snatch Ernestina away from her scoundrel of a husband, she left me. Went back to him! Her husband came looking for me one day and he broke down. He knelt and confessed that he was lost without Ernestina. Promise me you won't take her from me . . . Give me some water. I told him Ernestina and

I had parted ways some time before. And her husband said, she must have someone else then. We embraced and walked out into the street . . . when I met her she was wearing a red dress and had a daisy in her hair . . . we went from tavern to tavern; in every tavern, a swig. And then, surprise: At Papagai's, I met Faustina. He coughed, his voice growing hoarser as he spoke. And it was as though Ernestina had never existed. He lay there a while without opening his mouth, and when he said, I curse the day she let me enter her house, I thought his strength had given out, but he went on. The same day Faustina let me in her house and allowed me to kiss her behind the ear, she coiled around me like a snake. Straight away I explained it all to Ernestina's husband, and he told his wife. To Faustina I confessed that I had loved Ernestina and that her husband and I were like brothers . . . and I still don't know what happened, but shortly thereafter the four of us took to frequenting the taverns together: Ernestina friends with Faustina, Faustina friends with Ernestina's husband, and all three of them latching on to me. Not an hour went by that I didn't feel watched, spied on, my steps shadowed. It was me against the three of them . . . Them against me. Ernestina was defending Paulina one night when the four of us were walking down a street whose name I don't recall . . . I asked the hanged man who Paulina was and, after giving it some thought, he said he had misspoken, he had never known any Paulina and he meant to say Faustina, not Paulina . . . and I just couldn't take that kind of life any more, he continued. None of us made love, we had only reproaches for each other. I hated that dependency and yet I couldn't live without it. Until finally the war came and I enlisted right away in hopes of saving my soul. But the war has finished me. Emptied me of everything, surrounded me with death and blood . . . I died some time ago; why should I wish to breathe and possess a body that I despise and that persistently demands sleep, food, and sorrow? I mean joy, it asks for joy, even if just a little, but finds only sorrow . . . Why, why did you unhang me? He leaned in to punch me and fell backward as if I had punched him instead. I wrapped him in the sack and dragged him behind the rock, near the tree where he had hanged himself. Little by little I covered him with stones. I couldn't dig a hole to put him in because I didn't have a hoe, or a pick, or a mattock.

V

THE WAGON

THE BREAD THAT WAS LEFT IN THE HAVERSACK AND A FEW HAND-
fuls of blackberries I had picked nearby were my only meal that
day. I didn't know how to leave the dead man's side. It was late at
night when I lay down, with thoughts of Faustina and Ernestina
still in my head. I finally fell into a restless sleep, until daybreak
and the loud chirping of birds roused me. One of the birds had
an orange belly, the others had green bellies. A sparrow began
to squawk on the uppermost branch of the hanged man's tree. It
seemed to have gone mad. A song wafted up from the river; a girl
was singing. I looked down from my perch on the hanged man's
rock and saw a strip of blue water. The girl's voice had divested
me of my nocturnal memories. The voice grew loud at times, as if
the girl were facing the mountain as she sang; at times it darkened,
as if she had turned around. The sparrow continued to squawk.
For some reason it reminded me of my dead sisters. Perhaps because of that light, perhaps because the color of the sky that day
was the same color that drowsed in the carnation fields, perhaps
because . . . the oldest one was named Laieta, the middle one Lea
. . . the voice that drifted up from the river had gone silent. The
youngest was called Letícia, like my father's great-grandmother,
who was rich: She had two cars, six horses, wheat fields, a house
with twelve rooms and a dozen chimneys. All three girls had long
hair and dreamy, almond-shaped eyes. They were known in the

neighborhood as the three Ls. Laieta had a temper like a thousand demons; she died of a raging tantrum. She liked to be called just that, Laieta. Where's Laieta? What's Laieta doing? Is Laieta still in the garden? And that's when Mother, not wanting her to become capricious, started calling her La Lala. It made everyone laugh. La Lala. La Lala. But Laieta couldn't take it, and one day she broke into tears and started screaming, the blood vessels in her temples bulging, her mouth agape as she banged her head over and over against the wall. A vein in her neck burst and she collapsed to the floor as if she'd been steamrolled. The other two succumbed to disease. We buried them, each at her own hour, wearing their First Communion gowns that came down to their feet, with a crown of roses, a veil gathered about them like a cloud, and a rosary coiled around their arms . . . They were laid in caskets in the room with the red sofa, and when no one was keeping them company I would go and peep at them. They're going to heaven, Mother would say. They will all have gone to heaven. And when we get there, she would add with a blank expression, they'll come to greet us. I caressed their hands, neatly arranged across their chest; they were colder than the month of January. I straightened the crown of roses and studied the closed eyes that had looked at me so many times, glimmering like water. I would have liked to keep them with me forever; they were so still, so white, so free of malice.

I heard wagon wheels and men's voices approaching. I crouched among the shrubs and made my way to the bend in the road. Two wagons had just stopped. Three men got out of the nearest one, all of them bearded, disheveled, their shirts unbuttoned, wearing baldoliers and red scarfs around their necks. Bare legs ending in waxen feet, some bloodied, dangled from the back of the wagon farthest away. One of the men, the oldest, said he was famished. The other two, and the fourth man who jumped down from the wagon that was carrying the dead men, sat down on the ground. All of them had a knapsack. They dug their teeth into large hunks of cheese and long loaves of bread of a kind I had never seen before. They drank wine from a goatskin. The fat one with a ruddy face and a cleft nose cut the bread and cheese and distributed it. The youngest moaned that he didn't like cheese and would have preferred lamb chops. No one paid him any mind. The men said that the war might last a lot longer, maybe a hundred years. While there's cannon fodder, there will be war. A man who looked a bit like my father, but without the mustache, said that it was just the opposite: The war was coming to an end and it was only a matter of months . . . enough people had died; the country had been cleared of rabble. And rubble. Everyone laughed. The man with the cleft nose said, even if the war ends I'll never go home again. I'm sick and tired of always doing the same thing. Fed up with working the same hours every day, endlessly sweeping streets and squares. Me, said the one who craved lamb chops, I'm going to be a shepherd. A shepherd? You'll spend the rest of your life eating cheese. I'll kill the sheep! The sight of the men chomping away on their food made my mouth water, and I was swallowing saliva when someone gave me a shove and I tumbled smack into the middle of the group of men. Look at the rabbit I just caught! The man speaking had white hair and a wavy lock that fell across his brow. He had a shotgun slung over his back and wore corduroy trousers and boots that fastened on the sides with three buckles. They studied me as though I were a strange creature. Amusing ourselves by playing spy, are we? One of the men pinched my arm, so you, he said, you just decided to vamoose. I know you. We'd all do the same if we could, and let others break their backs. With that I took off running, but they caught up with me and dragged me back to the spot where I had fallen out of the bushes. The man with the split nose said, I've seen you before . . . Where did you stash those trousers you stole from Juli-Juli last night? He smacked me hard, with a hand that felt like iron. Spit it out: What'd you do with the trousers you stole? I swore I hadn't taken anyone's trousers. Oh yes you did they said, oh no I didn't I said, till I couldn't take it any longer and I just shouted: Liars! Big fat liars! For that I received two more blows that rattled my brain. Last night you crept into the barracks while he was sleeping and . . . I still had the energy to tell them I had spent the night watching over a man who had hanged himself. They all burst out laughing at that. A man who hanged himself? He says he spent the night with a hanged man. When I made as if to run away again—because when people don't want to recognize you're right, it's better to hit the road—the fellow who divvied up the bread and cheese really worked me over, while I shouted: Coward, coward! They left me fit for the dogs.

VI

The Girl by the River

Bits of cheese rind and three or four pieces of bread
crust had been left on the ground. I gobbled them down. I picked
some more blackberries and slowly made my way down to the
river. The water along the opposite bank wasn't blue, but green,
with clouds drifting by above it. I would have liked to be a river so
I would feel strong. I slipped into the water and swam like a fish,
no longer feeling the pain from the beating.

My father had cousins who lived on Carrer Atlàntida in Barcelona, in the neighborhood of Barceloneta, down by the sea. We
used to hunt for shells with their children and a girl by the name of
Mònica. I learned to swim and row with them. Before getting into
the water I ripped off the bandage on my arm; the flesh was purple
around the gash from the day I fell on a pile of broken bottles. On
the other side of the river lay an expanse of rushes and reeds, and
that is where I first saw her, more beautiful than life itself, standing
naked and holding a pitchfork. Her hair was the same ash blond
as mine was when I was little. A tiny waist, each thigh worthy of
respect—as my mother used to say of her carnations, each carnation worthy of respect—all of her a ripe peach. I slowly drew
closer; she spotted me, and when I reached her side she laughed
and poked me with the pitchfork. Her teeth were like little river
stones of the very whitest sort. The sun was starting to rise. The
reeds and leaves were swaying. She tossed the pitchfork aside and

25

dived into the water. I started swimming upstream and she followed behind me.

We lay in the sun and gorged on blackberries. She looked at me. Her violet eyes were dappled with gold, just like the eyes of the baby girl who got scratched by the cat, the one who lived near us and whose mother asked us to watch her. She said her father was a miller at the mill up the way; he was off at war and she only saw him on Sundays. As she spoke, I never stopped looking into her eyes. Her mother's name was Marta. Hers, Eva. She would have preferred to be a boy. She hunted birds with a slingshot. The fish that were too small when she caught them she threw back in the river; it was like giving them life and she liked that. Rabbits and partridges she hunted with a dog and a shotgun. If she had been a boy she would have gone off to war. She was aching to, but her father would have insisted on keeping her by his side and wouldn't have let her do what she wanted. Out of the blue she asked if I liked soap bubbles. The best thing about them was that, after one has waited so patiently to see them emerge from the tip of the reed and admire their iridescence, they burst while floating away, as if they had been pricked. She spoke lying down, with her hands behind her head, looking up at the sky. I wanted to touch her, to lay her on a bed of tender leaves plucked from violets. If this war that has already lasted so long lasts any longer I'll cut my hair, dress up like a boy, and join them. She stopped talking because on the opposite bank, farther downstream from the spot where I first saw her with the pitchfork, a man was passing by on the back of a donkey, a rifle across his back. It's my father, which means today is Sunday. It took us a while to raise our heads and by the time we did who could say where the miller was. A slender wisp of air toyed with us; we fell asleep as the moon was coming out.

She woke before me. When I opened my eyes she was no longer by my side; she was swimming. I followed her in. I couldn't resist grabbing hold of her foot; it slipped through my fingers like an eel. Get out! Three shadows were floating downstream. They're dead soldiers. To save themselves the trouble of burying, they hurl them off the cliff at Merlot. I prod them with the pitchfork so they won't get stuck and rot among the rushes and reeds that are my palace.

VII

The Miller Woman

We stopped near the mill, by the bridge across a bend in the river. Eva asked me to wait for her. She would come for me as soon as possible, but if she didn't I was to stay away from the mill. Just keep walking. I was hurt that she was leaving me. Here, I said, it's all I have, I want you to have it. I pulled the knife my father had given me out of my pocket and placed it in her hand.

Beneath the dense canopy of the old trees, with the dark river flowing below, I hardly breathed. One leaf, then another, grazed my cheek like the fingers of a corpse. Shards of moonlight allowed themselves to be carried off by the river. I thought I glimpsed shadows downstream. Someone in need of help. A voiceless someone. The piece of rope kept me company; I felt that those flimsy hemp threads protected me and I tightened my grip around them. The shadows drifting by were dead soldiers that the current had swept close to the reeds. They would cause the leaves to fall, they would cry out to the wind, they would grasp hold of whatever they could to keep the water from carrying them far from the place where they had died. Eva was taking a long time. She was not going to come. I walked on and on, until I chanced upon a well and hid behind it. I was almost to the mill. I could hear hinges squeaking, as though the wind that was just starting to pick up were flinging windows open and shut. All at once the large door to the mill swung outward, a stream of light emerged, and with it a white horse with a recumbent shadow on top. The horseshoes sent up sparks. Shortly thereafter a man appeared out of nowhere. Hunched under the weight of a sack, he entered a shed just as a blast went off in the distance, turning the edges of a cloud red. A truck was approaching; it stopped in front of the portal and two men alighted. The man who had entered the shed came out to meet them and they started unloading boxes.

Soon I heard shouts coming from inside the mill. I stood by the door, listening. A faint voice was saying that his horse, the horse he had left there to be tended, wasn't in the stable. A louder voice replied that he didn't know that the horse wasn't in the stable. Let them yell! A bag lay on the seat of the truck. My hand was still inside it, uncertain whether it had found an apple or a pear, when a blow to the back of my neck knocked me out.

$\sim\!\!\prec$

I strained to open my eyes. The rumble of a wheel turning had clouded my mind. Everything was in a haze until a few white patches began to take shape and I was able to make out the walls, the millstone . . . a pair of glassy eyes by my face. He's awake! a woman cried as she snickered and poured a bucket of water over me. The woman drew closer and struck me, kissing me as she hit me. We've got you now! She asked me my name while she kicked me in the side with the tip of her shoe. You can return my kisses on another occasion, you sewer rat . . . A white horse came to a halt by the portal. It walked over to where the woman stood, stopped, and started pawing the ground.

$\sim\!\!\prec$

I guess you know I'm the miller's wife, the woman said. I'm the mistress around here. My body had been covered with bruises since the day of the beating, the day of the hanged man. The woman uncovered me and started rubbing me with herbal oil. Poor little thing, so tender and so battered . . . As soon as she left me alone I tried to get up, but I couldn't stand.

I had lost all sense of time. The millstone turned and turned. The miller woman would come to check on me and talk nonsense. She didn't feed me. During the day she left a bottle of water by my side; at night there was nothing. He's a spy, I could hear them saying. A giant of a man scooped me up, took me to a large, empty room, and dropped me on the floor like a sack of potatoes. At night I could hear the truck, and there were arguments, the smell of smoke and oil, the sound of glasses clinking. During the day the miller woman would sprinkle flour over me; she found it amusing. The man who looked like a giant took me downstairs again and deposited me by the millstone. In the evening, the bats commenced their dance: They flew in and out and clustered together on the ceiling, in the corners, hanging like charred rags.

Today is Saturday, the miller woman said, staring at me as if wishing to pierce through me. Reclining beside me, she started to cover me with kisses. I tightened my lips and shut my eyes. I could have killed her. She finally tired, and with an angry voice she said when I stopped being such an idiot she would teach me how to make love. Have you ever made love? I summoned the strength to kick her in the stomach and she doubled over in pain. She threatened me with a raised fist. When my husband comes back—and he's probably crossing the bridge right now—you are going to get what's coming to you. When she heard him approaching, she started screaming that I was a shameless scoundrel. A scoundrel who pretends he can't even stand, but whenever I get near him . . . The miller, red as a chili pepper, eyes bulging out of his head, threw himself on me and started pummeling me while she stood there coldly, egging him on. Kill him! Kill him! When the man had had enough of beating me, he loaded me onto a wheelbarrow, carted me down to the river, and dumped me into the reeds, swearing such terrible things as I would have wished never to hear.

⤙

Some kind of animal drew near me. I turned over with a moan. The animal didn't budge. I stretched out my arm to touch it and felt an icy hand: I was lying next to a dead soldier. My bones ached, but I made an effort to overcome the pain and attempted to roll farther down the bank. The reeds stopped me. It was drizzling. I was starting to fall asleep, I couldn't understand why everything that was good in this world had abandoned me.

VIII

Like a Skeleton

I HEARD AN EXPLOSION COMING FROM THE DIRECTION OF THE
mill, followed by flames and plumes of smoke. Throngs of soldiers
were building a bridge across the river with rowboats and wooden
planks. The sound of engines and men shouting was deafening.
They must have worked all through the night. Soon trucks and
cannons were crossing the bridge, and the white horse—crazed,
neighing, rearing—stood in the middle of it all. Two silver planes
circled above the bridge. An explosion sent jets of water spewing
into the air. The bridge collapsed and four trucks fell into the river.
What are you doing here? You look like a skeleton. Juli-Juli stood
looking at me, shirt unbuttoned, face bloodied, hands trembling.
You escaped a real mess by hightailing it. He asked me what I had
done since I left. He was eager to talk, talk about anything. He sat
down beside me. Don't look. The water beneath the bombed bridge
has turned crimson. We're surrounded by dead soldiers. Talk as
much as you like, but don't look. Say something . . . quick. Don't
look toward the bridge. He laughed as he wiped the blood off his
face with his arm. He laughed louder, closed his eyes, opened them
again. His eyes were restless, never still. Did you know there's a
barmaid . . . she travels around in a wagon pulled by two horses
that are just flesh and bones. Hush, I said, covering his mouth with
my hand. Airplanes roared overhead; little by little the sound died
away. Her name's Faustina and she sells peanuts, belts with buckles

shaped like skulls, tobacco mixed with grass, and stale drinks. An ambulance approached the bridge. Through the reeds I caught a glimpse of the horse; it was standing still. The water was sweeping away dead soldiers, wounded soldiers, scraps of rowboats, burnt wood. Juli-Juli predicted that the war was winding down and we would soon be returning home, waving our flags amid throngs of girls who would throw flowers at us. It's in its final throes. Now we have to concentrate on saving our own skin. That, above all. He was quiet for a moment, and then he asked, have you ever flown? I fly at night. It keeps me from feeling hopeless. As soon as I lie down I imagine that, instead of a ceiling of reeds and plaster, above me there is the frenzy of the stars: trails of stars, fields upon fields of stars; and after a while of thinking only of the heavens, I start to float away and begin to fly. I see the mountains, the villages, the sea . . . all of it from up above. I had my eyes on the horse, which had started to move toward us . . . Then suddenly I couldn't breathe: Someone was poking me in the back. Two soldiers were standing behind me. Everything is going to pieces and the two of you are jabbering away. Animals! Yackety-yak. Without even entrusting myself to God or the devil, and risking being shot, I gathered the strength to make a dash for the horse and mount it. As if a spring mechanism had been released, it galloped furiously away with me on its back. Two shots rang out. One of the bullets raised a small cloud of dust a few meters from me. We passed through a forest, an abandoned village, a smoldering farmhouse; until the horse came to a sudden halt, sending me headfirst into a trench filled with water. I landed on top of Bartomeu, the cook for the soldiers I had left behind, just as he was emptying a machine gun on the men on the other side, shouting, try that on for size!

IX

LICE

THAT SAME AFTERNOON THE ORDER CAME TO WITHDRAW. JULI-
Juli gave me the news, though I still don't know how he found the
spot where the horse had thrown me. There were about a hundred
men, all of us young, bone-weary, bored. Our column did not stop
moving until we were within sight of an abandoned farmhouse surrounded by acacia trees, with a hill behind it. We climbed down
from the trucks and began setting up camp. The sense of peace that
pervaded the place made it seem as if the world had never been at
war. I learned to load and unload a rifle. To shoot. How old are
you? Fifteen. You look older. Come on, let's see if we can teach
you how to aim. I didn't want to. I aimed high or low, to the right
or the left of the cardboard man we were supposed to hit. I didn't
want to learn how to kill. The jerking of the rifle butt almost dis-
located my shoulder.

I got in the habit of climbing to the top of the hill to ease my
bouts of anxiety. Soon a Barcelona boy from the neighborhood of
Gràcia started joining me. His name was Agustí. He was born on
Torrent de les Flors; his family earned a living by selling milk. He
said everything at home had an odor of cow because the stable was
at the back of the shop. All those cows inside the house! He said
that after he was called up he had trouble sleeping without that
smell he had known since the day he was born. His mother would
wake him at four o'clock every morning to deliver the milk; he was

only eight years old then. With half-lidded eyes and a sleepy heart, he would traipse from one street to the next loaded with pans and measuring cups, sometimes climbing three flights of stairs in the dark to sell a lousy quarter of a liter of milk that only cost five cents. But at seven o'clock sharp he would put everything down: pans, measures, and all the other stuff, and he was off to Mass. The smell of incense overpowered him . . . the quietude, the priest's words that he liked because he didn't understand them. The chasubles thrilled him—white, rose, yellow, purple—every one of them embroidered in gold. And the lilies on the altar, the crowns of saints whose pink knees showed through a rip in their tunics. A neighbor complained to his mother that for days her husband had gone to work on an empty stomach because he hadn't delivered their milk; she knew it was on account of Mass. Every day to Mass. My mother, who kept a close watch on the business, slapped me silly and left me without dinner for two nights. But I sneaked down to milk a cow and drink the milk, gulping it down so fast in my haste to get back to bed that I almost choked. One's obligations above all else! my mother would shout. Piety above all else! declared Father Camilo at school, clasping his hands together, then opening his arms. I didn't know what to do, but I went to Mass even if it meant getting there in the middle and not being able to see the angel begin his work of covering the floor with little blue and crimson squares. Or seeing him blow the bubble that enveloped the church and created the petals that buttressed it all the way from the high altar to the last pew. What are petals? He looked at me: The leaves of plants are called leaves, the leaves of flowers are called petals. And he understood right away that because he had to deliver the milk he couldn't witness the scores of angels helping the first angel blow, while rays of light beamed from altar to worshippers and worshippers to altar. Feeling so bound by duty to my family made me want to cry, because it kept me from God who had made the churches. When I think that so many of them were burned down I want to kill the ones who did it, even if killing isn't allowed. And you—I asked him—who told you all that about the angel that blows and the bubble? He was silent for a moment and then said in a hushed voice, it's a secret. And, scratching his arm nervously, he added, here we go again: lice. Two days later I was also scratching myself. A shiver that started out sweet as honey and developed into a frenzy. After four days there wasn't a soldier left who didn't have his hair and every fold of his clothes mined with lice. Tiny ones, large ones, and eggs about to burst, white as chicken brains. Bartomeu said he could spot their flying shapes against the backlight. Juli-Juli said we thought about it too much. Kill 'em, but stop talking about it. We went down to bathe in a huge tank that collected water that gushed from a spring. But we couldn't rid ourselves of that plague of lice. They fly! I'm telling you they fly! With great parsimony, Juli-Juli squashed them between two fingernails. Whenever he caught an especially large one he would show it to us. Behold: A louse fit for a king! Lice were king there; they were glued to us and played possum when they had had enough. I saw one fly from Ximeno's shirt to Viadiu's back. They were eating us alive. Always ready to put their blood-sucking mouths to use. They don't have mouths, they have ducts!

One day, while it was still dark, five or six of us walked down the hill to bathe. I lingered behind the water tank, and then slipped away. The fighting had stopped, and it was as if the tranquility were spurring me to go in search of a place, any place, where I could rid myself of lice and soldiers.

⤚

There was no place where I felt good. Not in the fields, not beneath the trees, not inside the abandoned houses. Until finally, one after-noon, I saw just three steps in front of me a man in rags with white hair, beard too. He had a skull-shaped belt buckle. He sat down beside me without saying a word, removed two peaches from a dirty old basket—these are rainfed peaches—and handed me one. We looked each other in the eye, and I felt as if we had always known each other, as if I had met him—I didn't know where or when—one mid-afternoon much like that day's, sitting by the side of the road. As he bit into the firm, sugary flesh of the peach, he said without looking at me: The important things are the ones that don't appear to be important. More than wearing a crown, more than having the power to make the world bow at your feet, more than being able to touch the sky with your hands, above all else, there is this: ripe fruit into which you can sink your teeth by the fading light of day's end . . . look at that sunset! He tossed the pit as far as he could, wiped his lips with the back of his hand, and left me alone, my mouth filled with the taste of peach.

X

The Girl in the Two-Tone Dress

A LITTLE GIRL DRESSED IN GREEN AND RED, WITH CHOCOLATE-colored stockings, stopped in front of me as I was rubbing my face, which was just beginning to be covered with fuzz. She was carrying a basket chock full of Swiss chard. Juli-Juli had given me a shirt and a pair of trousers because the clothes I was wearing when we met again were in such a sad state, old and tattered. I never mentioned to him the lie about the stolen trousers, and he never said anything about it either. I don't know why, but, as the little girl studied me, I was glad I wasn't in rags. She stood in front of me, motionless, like a pine tree, looking at me with prying, adult eyes. She placed her basket on the ground and, before sitting down beside me, she brushed the sleeve of my shirt with her fingers. How sweet . . . I still had the peach stone in my mouth and didn't know what to do with it. What are you eating? I didn't reply. I took the stone with two fingers—when what I really wanted to do was to spit it out as far as I could—and threw it away. A farmhouse stood between us and a village that was a bit farther away. Is that your house? With a wag of the finger she indicated that it wasn't. I stood up slowly, as if I didn't want anyone to notice, and started walking; I realized at once that the girl was following me. She trudged along behind me, half dragging her basket of Swiss chard on the ground. The sun was at our back and the girl's shadow was small next to mine, like my sister Laieta's when I carried armfuls of carnations

to the front of the house to tie them in bunches of twelve. Are you
from that village? Yes. Are you lost? She set the basket on the
ground, pulled out a yellowing chard leaf and laid it at my feet.
How ugly, she said. I turned around and asked her where she had
found the chard—there weren't any vegetable patches around—
and why she ventured into the fields all alone and so young. She
didn't answer. She touched my shirt sleeve again, it's the color of
olives, she said as her lips made a little sound of admiration. She
maneuvered around to my left side and, taking me by the hand, she
said, Papà. We walked on, one step after the other. I'll take you
home, you can show me where it is. We approached the farmhouse.
An old woman sat at the entrance sorting lentils. She gave us a
dirty look and immediately lowered her head again and continued
working. After observing us for a while, a scrawny, docked-tail
dog tethered to a ring by a long, rusty chain began to bark. It jerked so hard on the chain as it barked that it risked choking to death.
Shut up! Shut up! We left the farmhouse behind and had scarcely
taken thirty steps when a boy bolted out of the house, racing in
the direction of the village as if the devil were on his tail. The village was an ancient one; the narrow street we headed up was paved
with river pebbles that formed a pattern. The houses had small
windows and every door had a peep window with iron bars across
it. Potted plants hung down over the balconies, green with crimson blooms. Everything held the stench of manure and the smell of
carobs. Leaning out of a window, a girl with wet hair and a towel
around her neck stared at us and spat just as an old peasant woman
dressed in black stepped out of her house carrying two chickens
by the feet, their crests redder and curlier than the flower of the
pomegranate tree. When she caught sight of us, she stormed back
inside and slammed the door. The young boy from the farmhouse

ran toward us shouting, his face contorted with rage, they're here! They're here! There was an instant uproar. Child snatcher! You're not going to take this one the way you did the other! She's a relative of the deceased mayor. He should be lynched! Hang him! Old men and younger men with sticks and pitchforks were coming up the street toward us. She's a relative of the mayor. Hang him. Hang him. Without thinking twice, I let go of the little girl's hand that had begun to clasp mine tighter and tighter, and I ran for it. I ran from the village, across a dry riverbed and a field as flat as the palm of my hand. My flight was halted by a ravine that I followed until the village behind me started to resemble the village in a Nativity scene. Just as I was turning around to wave goodbye to it, I tripped over some legs and fell flat on the ground.

XI

THE RELIGIOUS MEDALLIONS

THE MAN SLEEPING BY THE DYING FIRE HAD NOT BUDGED. IN THE light of the embers and the fading day, his face looked sweaty, ringed by hair that was part yellow, part some unknown color. His upper cheeks were marked with red streaks and his nose was covered with warts. A thread of saliva oozed from the corner of his mouth. His shins were coal black. He was sleeping on his side on a cushion of grass. As I watched him, he opened his eyes and closed them again. He was heaving, his bronchi clogged with cobwebs. There was a smell of coffee. I found some in a pot and poured it into an empty tin that was lying about. Almost as if those two sips of coffee had been poppy nectar, I fell asleep immediately. People began parading through my spirit, a never-ending procession determined to march up and down. The procession finally entered my house, paying no mind to where it treaded and crushing all the carnations. I kept thinking: They know not what they do. When I awoke, on the summit of an unfamiliar peak, atop some unnamed mountain—real or of fog—an icy moon the color of seashells was shining high above. A meteor shower swept across the sky. I had never seen one before. The stars are weeping because we are at war, said the old man, who had sat up. He seemed to have always known me. The stars fell at a slant; the wind at such heights must have kept them from falling straight down. Many dissolved in midair, others reached the ground. Some were pink, some bluish. They have grown weary of seeing so much death. I've always heard, I told the man, that a meteor shower is a harbinger of war; I would never have thought I would see one when there has been a war going on for so long. There are all kinds of meteor showers: those that herald war and others, like this one, that could mean that a war is unfolding and who is to say when it will end . . . everyone knows when a war starts, son, but no one can be certain when it will end. Even little children know that, I said. What do you mean? That what is known to everyone isn't worth repeating. I've come to realize that people talk just to hear their own voices and they always say the same thing. And how would you like things to be? I'd like for people to speak only the things worth saying and nothing more. If you didn't know it already, it's worth remembering that life is repetition. Why don't you want people to repeat themselves when they talk? Because I find it tiring. So then you shouldn't like yourself either, as you are nothing more than a repetition yourself. I haven't liked myself for years. I am annoyed by my own self. Everything about me annoys me, starting with my hair and all the way down to my feet . . . including this spot on my forehead. I'd rather be a plant, the kind that sprouts and sprouts without realizing it's alive. But they do realize they're alive; they know in which direction to turn to draw more light and sun, and those that need shade know to turn toward the shade. And seeds always find a way to plant themselves and take root where they should. A mountain plant would never choose to grow in a garden. And if a man moves it to a garden it will die of sadness . . . More coffee? How did you know I'd already had some? I always sleep with one eye open, the way hares do; I find that in order to sleep soundly I need to have a hare's fear about me. We drank coffee, I from my tin and he from a dented pan. I asked him how he managed to procure it, because it wasn't much of a stretch to say that we hadn't seen any at home since the war began. From a tattered suitcase he removed a paper cone. He had a roguish gleam in his eyes. Thanks to my religious medallions. Many grocers and many soldiers who are the sons of grocers are still believers. They purvey the coffee and I give them religious medallions in exchange. Mine are the most beautiful. An old woman who lives in the middle of the forest, near the river, makes them; she's a real beast, worse than ringworm. Look at these—they represent Our Lady of the Angels. You see? Take a good look at them. The Virgin's dress is lovely, every bit of it is stunning, but I don't know how she manages to have the Virgin's faces look as evil as her own. I'll give you some so a bullet won't cut you down. Keep them with you always; perhaps some nights you will hold them for a while, and because you will believe in the good fortune they bring, you will be lucky. Remember my words . . . We fell asleep with the Big Dipper above us. At dawn there was no sign of the medallion peddler, but around my neck hung images of Our Lady of the Angels holding a blooming lily with seven buds. Soon, even more shell-hued than the previous night's moon, the new day awoke to eyes that have never tired of seeing the tenderness it brings.

XII

EVA

THE HENHOUSE WAS AT THE BACK OF THE VEGETABLE GARDEN. I
crept toward it, like a wolf stealing through the artichokes. A hen
was clucking like mad. I would eat her egg. The frightened fowl
stood over her nest, legs deep in the straw, staring at me. The
egg tasted like hazelnuts. Three more hens, still as death, craned
their necks forward as they perched on their nests. Their wattles
drooped, their combs drooped, they were old hens, had laid many
eggs, marched many little chicks around. I heard the sound of a
slamming door coming from the direction of the house, followed
by the squeak of a pulley. The egg had made me hungry. I left the
vegetable garden. There wasn't a village in sight. I was surrounded
by fields. I was suddenly struck by a flash of sadness, and I shook
it off in a hurry. Somehow, I would find what I needed. I continued
on my way, slit-eyed, blinded by a sun that had a deeper yolk color
than the egg I had just swallowed. I was walking in the bright sunlight, my mind on other things, when I tripped and fell, bloodying
my knee. The blood was red, redder than a red carnation, redder
than the drooping combs of those golden hens.

In an effort to take my mind off my hunger, I tried to get some
sleep by the side of the road, among the weaver's broom. In an

effort to take my mind off my hunger and hoping that someone
might pass by, like the old man with the peach . . . I was dreaming
I was little and wasn't walking yet, that I was watching a stopped
train that was very long and shrouded in fog . . . when someone
took my hand. It was a friendly hand. A hand in the middle of a
river with banks graced by rushes and reeds. That hand was Eva,
the whole of her; she had spotted someone lying on the ground,
wounded perhaps, and had come to help. She was clad in militia overalls, boots, a faded sweater, and a cap. Those violet eyes
looked at me as though looking at the world and everything good
in it, and that notion sent a wave of shame rushing to my cheeks.
She said observing me had calmed her heart. She had seen so many
people lose their lives that sometimes when she thought of me she
pictured me dead and that pained her . . . dead in the attack on the
mill that belonged to her parents who were not her parents. She
had chosen her real parents; they were the Sky and the Earth, he
laden with stars, she with flowers. I wanted to ask her if she had
been the one riding the white horse out of the mill that night, and
why she had told me down by the river that if she were a boy she
would go off to war, and why—being a girl—she had gone to war,
and why she hadn't said as much when we got to the bridge and
she told me to wait for her. I wanted to ask her how she knew that
the mill had burned down . . . But I didn't say anything because
she sat down beside me and, leaning to the side, drew the knife I
had given her from her pocket and showed it to me, it's broken,
she said. I tried to open a box using the screwdriver as a lever, and
there you have it, a broken screwdriver. She was happy to see me
again; in a low voice, she added that she had never liked people
who loved her. To love her was to shackle her, it didn't allow her
to move. She needed to be herself and be free to go wherever she

wanted and help whomever she wanted, without the sense that doing so was an obligation. I like you . . . because you don't tie me down and because of that look you have on your face. I've only been with you for a few hours but I've always remembered you; I think of you often, even if I don't see you. We met in the water . . . She remained silent for a while; I couldn't take in everything she was saying. Sometimes my nature is to run away . . . the dead are the only ones who don't frighten me. They ask for nothing; that's why I feel sorry for them, and love them, especially because I sometimes think that I'm more dead than alive . . . if things made any sense I would have died lives and lives ago, mine and other people's lives . . . They have to be buried deep in the ground so they can rest forever close to the roots. And become trees.

She let go of my hand and I felt a pang of abandonment. She looked down at the ground for a while and then, without lifting her eyes, she explained that she had taken three badly wounded soldiers to a field hospital at the army's rearguard so they could die in peace. They were young like you, with as much desire to live as you have. See that Red Cross truck by the shrubs? There's a cross on the sides and on the roof of the truck. See the red of the cross? When I was little my father killed a cat, I don't know what it had done to him; I witnessed it and it broke my heart. I buried it in the early morning by the bridge where I told you to wait for me. Remember, the day we met? I made a cross of red flowers on top of it. And some evenings, when the setting sun is ringed by clouds and sends fanlike rays of light to Earth, I see myself climbing upward along the ribs of the fan, the cat by my side, glancing at me from time to time . . . and . . . what's that?

She noticed the cord I had around my neck and tugged on it. You're wearing religious medallions? She laughed. She pushed her cap back and it fell to the ground. She wore her hair shorter than I did when I was a young boy. It's Our Lady of the Angels, I said. She studied the medallions for a while. She's so ugly . . . it would give me the creeps to wear such an ugly Virgin Mary around my neck. I said: A wise man gave them to me and told me that as long as I wore them no bullet could kill me. She laughed again and, before standing, she leaned toward me and kissed the birthmark on my forehead. Want to come? I shook my head. Soon I heard a truck engine. In the waning light I glanced at the embroidered Mother of God. The dresses, lilies and leaves all had lovely colors, but I didn't want to look at the medallions because the Virgin bore the face of that hideous old woman. I removed them from around my neck and put them in my pocket; but first I superimposed Eva's face over the old woman's hideousness. Want to come? No. I said no to please her. Had I not seen the crushed grass where Eva had sat, I would have believed that Eva and Eva's kiss had just been one of those dreams from which you never wish to awaken.

XIII

The Farmhouse

A GIRL A LITTLE OLDER THAN THE GIRL WITH THE SWISS CHARD
emerged from a bakery carrying a round loaf of bread with a dark
brown crust. She started skipping and the bread tumbled to the
ground and ended up almost at my feet. Without giving it a thought
I grabbed it and ran. I didn't even turn around when I heard the
girl shouting. That bread never again saw the light of day. At the
first fountain I drank my fill of water. Soon I was bloated. As I sat
on the ground, my hands holding my aching belly, several trucks
carrying soldiers passed by, followed by three wagons pulled by
mules. The fighting was close-at-hand. My heart told me to make
my way to the road, my head told me to flee. I didn't feel like moving but I had to go somewhere. Perhaps as I roamed from village
to village the war would end and when it was over . . . A pair of
espadrilles was drying on a windowsill. Mine had lost part of the
soles. I crouched down and crept over to the window. I put on the
espadrilles behind a hedge, they were just my size. I walked on
calmly. Soon a farmhouse with three haystacks by the threshing
floor came into view. On one side there were only fields, on the
other, rows and rows of olive trees. Pink carnations hung from the
middle balcony of the house. I heard shouting and threw myself on
the ground. You vile thing! Miserable rascal! A short, fat man was
beating a whimpering dog that cowered beneath him. When the

man tired of striking the dog, he turned and left it there without even a glance, grumbling as he went. The mangled dog dragged itself over to me, its tail tucked between its legs, snout trailing along the ground, and licked my hand. It was a large black dog, with blond fur on its underside. It lay down beside me with a sad sigh. If he dies tonight, I thought, I'll bury him.

—≺

It had turned dark. From the farmhouse came the smell of rich soup. I crept closer, lured by the smell, until I was standing in the middle of the portal in a stupor, begrudging them the food. The farm woman noticed me right away. She opened her mouth, but no shout emerged from it. The farmer turned his head: His face was the color of the earth, and he had a dark beard and hair cut so short it resembled a brush. Staring at me like a pair of owls, two twin girls with spoonfuls of soup halfway to their mouths were fighting back laughter, as if amused that I was so filthy and that my always-empty stomach was flatter than a carpet beater. With a thunderous voice, the farmer ordered me to come in; he had me tell him where I was from and what my name was. I explained I was lost, I had been separated from the other soldiers by clouds of smoke after a series of explosions. He told his wife to serve me a bowl of soup. The dish was deep, glazed, its rim decorated with painted flowers, which I kept my eyes on as I ate, seated on the stone hearth because the farmer had not asked me to sit at the table. I could have eaten seven whole pots of that rich, warm soup. They gave me two slices of bread larger than my feet, and I kept dipping them in the soup. I saw that the farmer had a wooden leg, which I hadn't noticed when he was whipping the dog. He asked me what I planned to do. Rejoin the soldiers, I said. There's time for that. Around here we have more work than we can manage. So, not feeling inclined to start roaming again from place to place, I stayed. They had me wash the dishes and showed me where I would be sleeping: a tiny alcove with a cot and a stool, just beside the hearth. You entered through a small door that didn't shut well and had a crack in the middle, so if you put your eye to it from the outside, you could see the cot. I pushed the cot against the wall that had the hearth on the other side. The family slept upstairs. I was still working in the kitchen when they went up and left me alone. After I washed the soup pot, I hid the bones in it and then dumped them in a bucket under a pile of potato skins and cabbage leaves.

—⟨—

The night was sweet, blue-black, yet lighter around the edges of the moon. Bucket in hand, I went in search of the dog. I had trouble finding him. He was lying against a low drywall on the edge of a field, his breathing belabored. Without touching him I set the bones down near him, and I saw his eyes gleaming.

—⟨—

After a fortnight at the farmhouse, I had recovered to such an extent that when I studied my image in the goose pond I scarcely recognized myself. I ate mountains of potatoes, heaps of rice, bowls and bowls of pork and vegetable stew. One day the farm woman— her name was Fermina, pale skinned, with moist, sleepy eyes like the dog that was beaten—told me that her two sons, Miquel and

Llorenç, had died in the war, after all the effort it had taken to bring them up. Why did they have to die? And who did they die for? She had watched the boys go. She could still see them: two shadows silhouetted against the glory of the sun. Every evening since that day she would stand in the doorway, gazing at the mountains, waiting and waiting, sick with yearning. With tears in her eyes she confessed that I and her youngest son, Miquel—who was an angel—were like two drops of water from the same fountain, so much did we resemble each another.

I had to work hard. I couldn't handle it all: pulling up potatoes, tilling the vegetable garden and watering it . . . You're doing a good job. I told them about our field of carnations. I had to carry the baskets of laundry to the clotheslines, clean the stable, henhouses, pigeon coop, and rabbit cages, and provide fodder to the old horse with a sore on its left hip that was always covered with flies. I had to wash the dishes, kill hens and chickens, chop wood and pile it up all neat for when the great cold arrived. The only chore the farm woman did not task me with was collecting eggs, because, as she made plain to me, she was afraid I would drink them raw the way Miquelet did; he would suck as many as he could in one sitting, and if the family wanted to have an omelet they had to go buy eggs at the next farmhouse, and each omelet cost them forty eggs. The farmer spent most of his time in the village, glued to a bench in the tavern playing cards . . . Little by little the dog began coming closer to the farmhouse; if he caught sight of the farmer, who never even looked at him, the dog bared his teeth and the hair on his back stood up. I always left food for him by the same wall as that first time, and he always waited for me there. After he had eaten, he would sit next to me and the two of us would look at the moon.

He was always right there behind me, never leaving my side. He was my greatest companion; we loved each other.

I felt spied on by the twins. The firstborn was named Teresina. The second-born was called Camineta—little walker—because, apparently, as soon as she was born she wiggled her legs as if wanting to walk. Teresina told me that her father had beaten the dog because it had stolen a piece of ham and nothing infuriated him more than thieves. But in reality, they were the ones who had taken the ham. When their father noticed that the ham was missing, the girls blamed the dog and escaped a good thrashing. They burst out laughing as if they had gone mad.

A dull rapping on the wall by the hearth woke me. I pulled on my trousers and opened the door. It was the twins, who started laughing as they always did when they saw me. Camineta, wearing tiny gold earrings, whispered to me to go with them; they needed my help. She was carrying a small lantern. We went up to the second floor, holding onto the banister as we tiptoed up the steps. They led me to a large room that had the sweet scent of lavender. We climbed a ladder that was propped against a hole in the ceiling and entered the attic. The smell there could not be easily described. From the ceiling hung strings of garlics and bunches of onions. I stumbled on a heap of potatoes while trying to avoid some sacks of wheat, the contents of which were waiting to be transferred into large boxes scattered around the room. A rabbit pelt, dry and badly hung, brushed against my cheek. Everything was burning hot. The twins stopped in front of a huge armoire that reached all the way to the ceiling. Slide it away from the wall. Holding up the lantern, Camineta pointed to the bulky object. Move it back without making any noise. I tried to move it, tried with all my strength, but it wouldn't budge. I kicked it. No noise, I said! Teresa glared at me, her eyes filled with fire. I braced my back against one side of the wardrobe, my feet solid on the ground, and pushed with all my might. It was useless. With Camineta behind me shining her light for me, I searched every corner for a tool I could use as a lever. A long board did the trick: I slid it behind the wardrobe and succeeded in moving it forward a bit. If we shift it a couple of spans, Teresina said, we'll be able to get into the larder: The door behind the wardrobe opens inward. Suddenly I had the impression that the armoire was slipping and was about to topple on me. If you make any noise, it's all over. Father will wake up—he sleeps just below us—and none of us will live to see the dawn. Bam! One of the doors to the armoire had swung open. The inside was filled with sacks of rice. Let's empty it out. We went about it like hired hands employed to remove the sacks and dump them on the floor. After that it was easy to move the armoire. The room Teresina called the larder occupied the entire top floor of the farmhouse, and it was chock-full of food. From the beams hung hams, dried sausages, blood sausages, white sausages, and *sobrassada* sausages. Camineta showed me around. Bet you didn't expect this. Large vats of olive oil. Huge jars filled with lard, balls of fat clustered together, as large as the heads of babies. Crocks of confit: goose, turkey, rabbit, chicken. Teresina, perched on the top of a ladder with a pair of scissors she produced from who knows where, started cutting at the rope that was holding a ham. Right away she started carving it up and dishing it out: it was dry, it was salty, it was good.

Although we never went hungry, we devoured it as if we were starving. In a corner, apples, persimmons, and figs were scattered about on top of sacks . . . We left taking with us the remainder of the ham and pushed the armoire back in place, leaving everything as we had found it.

⌣

The following night I wasn't able to take the dog any food. I heard footsteps going up and down the stairs. The wooden steps creaked; there were muffled, incensed voices, and the atmosphere was permeated by a strange disquiet that for a long time wouldn't let me close my eyes. I woke from a restless sleep, and rather than the usual thread of light streaming through the crack in the door, I saw the door ajar and the farmer's shadow in the middle, holding an ash rod. His eyes were fixed on the ham that was on my pillow. He dragged me from the bed, and once he had me out on the threshing floor he began to beat me with the same rage I had seen him use on the dog. With every lash he shouted in a hoarse voice, you little thief! You thief! At one point I raised my head and saw the twins leaning over the balcony with the pink carnations, poking each other with their elbows and snickering. Suddenly the thrashing stopped. The dog had pounced furiously on the farmer and sunk his teeth into the man's neck.

⌣

The forest was thick with small-leaved trees and yellow, moss-covered rocks that were piled into mounds. I lay by the rocks, without the strength to think. A scorpion was crawling in my direction, its stinger raised: It moved slowly but was headed straight for me. In the time it takes to say "Amen," a large black bird swooped down and carried it off.

XIV

A Night in the Castle

I HID IN THE DAYTIME AND MADE MY WAY AT NIGHT. ONE EARLY morning, half-starved, I came upon a carrot patch. It was wonderful to tread on so many green leaves. They weren't fully grown carrots, but tender as water, sweeter than honey. "If you play rabbit, I'll fill you so full of lead you'll never get up again." A ruddy-faced man standing at the edge of the forest was aiming his shotgun at me. "Rabbit! Rabbit!" I bolted from the field as if I were being pursued and had the hunter's dog on my tail, crossing fields, crossing vineyards, until I reached the foot of a hill at the top of which stood a castle. The sea lay before me, a festival of waves.

Not far from the beach, a whale-shaped rock was awash with crabs. I was too exhausted to go and collect some. I climbed the hill and sat with my back against a castle wall full of crevice-dwelling lizards. I heard voices singing a song about rifles and bullets. Through some lavender bushes I spotted the heads of two young men: One was bald, the other had a shock of black hair. Both were missing an arm: The one on the right had no left arm, the one on the left was missing his right arm. Without interrupting their song, they sat down with their backs to me, a good bit below the spot where I was. Their rucksacks appeared full. I couldn't see what they were eating. They drank straight from the bottle. The black-haired guy wiped his mouth and asked: Did Isabel cry much? Shut up. She must have cried a lot. Shut up. I didn't think you could possibly leave her . . . I don't want to marry without an arm. I returned the postcard with the pomegranate. The one with the black hair said, when the war's over we'll look for a lame fellow who can play the guitar and we'll sing about her as we make the rounds of the villages. We'll tell people we laughed at the bullets and the bombs. The other replied, I will mourn my arm for the rest of my life. I will be consumed by rage, the whole of me a bag of envy. Don't think about your arm. We'll sing, and our singing will quicken people's hearts and rouse their minds. They finished eating and walked by without seeing me.

The stone wall was warm from the sun. I paused by the portal. The courtyard was large, with brambles in the corners. By a well lay a tattered flag, its pole broken, and a tangle of blood-smeared sheets. The stained glass in three high windows was ablaze with light. The wind picked up and the panting of waves reached me. The entrance to the castle was a dark mouth with a staircase at the end. Three doors gave onto the landing. I chose the middle one. The room seemed to have been built for giants, with a hearth for giants. Another room followed with a table in the middle in the shape of a counter; some thirty iron soldiers armed with lances were positioned between the huge windows and on either side of the doors. Another room, resembling a corridor, had twelve windows facing the sea; the opposite wall was covered with bits of broken mirror. As I was studying the wall that shattered me to pieces as though I were merely a composite of shards, I noticed the scent for the first time: the smell of the yellow roses from our rosebush at home that climbed all the way up to the railing on the rooftop terrace.

A stairway with only a few steps led straight to a small door. I opened it. The room was dark, merely a box with neither window nor balcony. The door slammed shut behind me. With my back to the wall, I scarcely dared to breathe; I heard footsteps approaching, someone walking with the help of a cane. Clack, clack, clack . . . The wall I was leaning against swung ajar and I spied a room in penumbra; there was only the light of a hearth. A man seated in an armchair was looking straight at me. Come in. He had sunken eyes, a long beard, and gnarled hands. A pistol lay on the table in front of him. After telling me to sit, he began to speak. The castle has had many visitors, some who wanted to kill me, others who wanted to save me. Between the two, everything I possessed has been taken from me. No more tapestries or valuable, centuries-old furniture . . . but I wept most for the loss of the sun . . . he pointed to a large nail in the middle of the hood above the hearth, it once hung there, solid gold, larger than my belly. It had a face with a mouth, eyes and nose. Are you listening? Just by reaching out your arm, you could kill me. The gun is loaded. I could also kill you. It must be a grand thing to stem a life that is just beginning, but I won't because you have that stunned animal expression, and stunned animals have always evoked my respect because of the world's great need for them. Look, there are some things I need to say: Wise men should not weep for the living or the dead . . . Youth is always sad, and it always rests in other people's hands . . . He took my hand. Youth is for stroking wood, stone, the tender skin of one's first love. Even before sunrise, the sun already knows that it is the sun, and that the dew has been waiting for it long before daybreak, waiting even before it was born. He let go of my hand. The wall at the back of the hearth glimmered, as did the eyes of the old man seated in his chair. In every man we find deep roots that bind him to the great symphony of the world . . . I tiptoed out of the room. I crept along, staying close to the wall, finding only closed doors, lightless windows, stairs. All at once, the moonlight illuminated a corner where shadows lay across the floor. I heard groans. I did not know where I was. The bolts on the doors that I tried to open were all rusty . . . until finally one yielded . . . and a strong hand grabbed me by the ankle. I managed to smother the cry that was about to emerge from my throat.

XV

THE PRISONER

I AM IMPRISONED HERE UNTIL THE END OF MY DAYS. I AM THE master of this castle. It was seized from me by a distant relative from a poor side of the family, whom my parents took in while still a child. Everything I had, he had as well. But he was envious of me, and the envy that festered within him could have filled seven wells. With smiles and gentle manners he earned my trust; he was my most beloved friend. But then, as soon as the war began, he robbed me of everything I had. First the gold sun, then the two chalices encrusted with diamonds, rubies, and emeralds, and the candelabras adorned with moonstones. The castle chapel was emptied of valuables. Despoiled of saints, altars, retables, crown-bearing angels. People were paid to loot and rob, taking all the silver and gold, the tapestries with scenes of war, of hunting parties, of raging seas, of love. When armed men arrived at the castle, he turned me over to them to avoid being killed himself, telling them he was the poor one, I the rich. He had my knees broken. I lay for God knows how long in the open grave where the bodies of the executed were dumped. Dragging myself, my belly to the ground like a snake, I was able to make it back to the castle. The hatred in his eyes when he saw me was spine-chilling. His threatening figure towered over me as he looked at me and said that as punishment he would not allow me to die. I was brought to this dark room. Sometimes he brings me food. Other times he forgets. I never see him. He knows how to choose the moment of one's sleeping death. Feel no pity for me. Do not try to save me. Perhaps I have the punishment I deserve for my lust, for having believed myself more powerful than God. He has made himself the master of my discernment; he has become my lord. I live for him and through him. I am him. I am his wickedness, his cruelty. My prison is not these walls, but my own flesh and bones. Never allow yourself to be defeated. He paused for a moment, then continued in a changed tone. Observe and admire the perfect order of the stars, the passing of time with its retinue of seasons: the gates of summer, the gates of winter. Observe the waves, attend to the grandeur of the winds that the angels blow from the four corners of the pulsating heavens. The lightning that streaks everything with fire, the crawling thunder . . . I adored rosy cheeks, turgid buttocks, honey-sweet breasts, dawn-colored thighs, snow-white, nacreous feet . . . Books that impart wisdom, blazing sunsets from my windows, the pearly light of the night star. My life had been a perfect jewel, a diamond. What are my broken bones but a way of binding me to the realm of memories, to everything I once had and still retain because it dwells in the darkest recesses of my heart? Tell me, where are the nymphs of old, surrounded by lilies and the water that flows through the deep umbrage of my woodlands, weaving garlands of nightshade, sleeping in dark grottos resonant with the cries of love lost? My flesh is tired, my skin as brittle as glass. I sleep on the floor surrounded by tranquil spiders and the dust that I ingest, the dust that I am and that I will become when, far from the blue cries of the sirens, a blinding light will welcome me to the land of the pure. Pray, pray always that man might behold the marvelous abundance granted him so that he might not destroy it or fling it into the abyss of terror where everything freezes over . . .

Half deranged by the words of that madman whose face I had not even glimpsed, I crawled backward, too filled with dread to turn my back to him. And with the sound of his strangely sweet voice still ringing in my ears I found myself rolling down a viscous slope. When I got to the bottom, I tried to stand. My arms could reach from one wall to the other. I crept along the sewer line until a breath of fresh air hit me and I lost consciousness.

XVI

Three Girls and an Orange

Look, there's a boy at the mouth of the sewer line from the castle. Is he dead? If he were dead his face would be paler. The voices reached me from afar, slowly waking me. They were the voices of girls. Of girls standing around me. Then a shadow leaned down and something soft, perhaps a blade of grass, perhaps a feather, grazed my cheek. I couldn't stand the tickle. Don't give him any love pats. I could see six feet, six legs, six knees. Three girls were observing me, amused. He has one eye open, he's just pretending to sleep. See how it shines? I sat up, and the girls ran away, laughing and shrieking. A flight of seagulls circled above them. The shrieking girls with their feet in the water, and the seagulls on that bright morning transported me to a very different world. An orange soared through the air. The girls were playing, tossing it back and forth. Nice and round, it surged upward against the blue and then fell swiftly into the two hands at the end of two arms that awaited it. From behind a rock that prevented me from seeing her fully, another girl, who looked like a figurine in a Nativity scene, was approaching. All of her, I later noticed, was the color of a camellia flower; she had large, black eyes and thick hair that fell down her back. The other girls immediately surrounded her. One who was very blonde asked: Are you still crying over him? Forget him. If he wants to travel the world singing, let him, and wish him well. Her fiancé left her? asked the girl who was wearing a yellow blouse. Yes. Isabel was so afraid he would be killed in the war, but it only took one of his arms. And now he says he doesn't want to marry with just one arm. The figurine girl started explaining to the girl in the yellow blouse what the others already knew. Her fiancé's father was a blacksmith and he, the son, was strong and brave; he used to help his father forge iron. Hammer and anvil were all sparks . . . I moved closer to them. The figurine girl glanced at me, and I don't know what she saw in my eyes but as she looked at me hers moistened. The blonde girl said, Isabel loved him very much. We've known each other since we were little and used to play in front of the castle, making paper boats out of newspapers. Then we'd go down to the beach and float them on the water, lying facedown on the crab rock. The figurine girl looked at me again, and again it seemed that her eyes and mine had no wish to hold any other gaze. So now you know the whole story: He doesn't want to marry with one arm, it doesn't matter that I've waited for him for so long, dreamed of him for so long. My mother is happy: What would you do with a one-armed cripple for a husband? You'll find another who's better, richer and has the right number of arms and hands . . . The figurine girl started running toward the waves screaming that she wanted to die. They took her farther down the beach, and the girl in the yellow blouse walked over to me and tossed me the orange.

XVII

THE MAN WITH THE SANDWICH

A MAN CAME AND STRETCHED OUT BESIDE ME. HE WAS PORTLY and his skin glistened as if it had been smeared with lard. He folded his hands over his belly. I could only see one of his eyes, beneath an eyebrow with hairs thicker than esparto. The eye studied me, then quickly closed, only to open again slowly. To escape its scrutiny I pretended to gaze at the sky. There were still seagulls in flight; two had come to rest on the rock with the crabs. The man had placed between us a bundle made from a large striped kerchief. Would you untie the bundle and hand me the sandwich? he muttered. It was a huge sandwich with cured ham spilling out of the sides. I can't say I'm hungry, but one gets an appetite by eating. I handed him the sandwich but straight away he gestured that he didn't want it. No, no . . . put it in my mouth. He opened his mouth: rotting teeth, a short, fleshy tongue covered with white fuzz, the uvula red as fire. I lowered the sandwich to his mouth and he closed it parsimoniously, taking his first bite. The smell of the tomato-rubbed bread and the ham was driving me mad. I let the sandwich drop to the ground, crouched with my nose to the sand, and dug my teeth into the crust. A good long piece of ham pulled out. What are you doing? I can't see you. I didn't dare chew, didn't dare say a word with my mouth full. Dry my lips for me. There's no more ham? Put what's left of the bread in my mouth, tiny morsels. And stuff the kerchief in my pocket. He was silent and seemed to be half asleep, but then he started talking. His voice, my hunger, the ebb and flow of the sea were making me drowsy. He spoke about his life, at times looking up at the sky, at others closing his eyes. Sometimes his words came out broken. I've been ti . . . red for as long as I can re . . . mem . . . ber, since I was born. I might as well tell you the whole story. My mother was unable to nurse me because I wouldn't suckle, and if I did, I suckled so slowly that she was forced to spend hours holding me. She fell behind on the housework: clothes always dirty, beds unmade, dishes unwashed. Until, at her wits' end, she decided to feed me straight from the bottle. Two neighbors were in charge. One of the women opened my mouth, the other stuck the neck of the bottle in and milk spewed out. I cried, I choked, I suffocated. My mother used to say, I still don't know why he didn't die. I didn't walk till I was five years old, if you can call that walking. I had to sit down every couple of steps, I would fall asleep all over the place. Four steps and a nap. I was rejected for military service because I kept nodding off. They said my sleepiness was caused by a disease of the brain. My wife is called Narcisa, and we hadn't been married three months when she got into bed with the assistant to Senyor Regomir, the lawyer. That's how it is. I never take off my trousers. Why should I if the following day I have to put them on again? He was quiet for a moment. A soot-colored cloud hastened to hide the sun. The seagulls seemed whiter. The lethargic man slept. A bee circled the cavity of his mouth. I rose, glancing in the direction of the castle to see if there truly was a castle by the beach. When I had walked for a while, I turned around to take one last look at it, but it had receded from view. The wide sea was leaden.

XVIII

THE GIRL ON THE BEACH

I SAW SHIMMERING LIGHTS IN THE DISTANCE. THERE WOULD BE poorly guarded chicken coops, egg-laying hens, fruit-laden trees. To my left, a tiny, bright speck hovered above the water: a butterfly. A gentle hand took me by the arm. A girl's voice asked: Why were you looking at me? The face was pale, partially covered by a cascade of hair. The butterfly drew nearer and nestled into it. Why were you looking at me? It was dark but I could see the wings of the butterfly, seemingly dead. I picked it up and it stayed in the palm of my hand. You silly thing, I wanted to tell her. I tossed the butterfly into the air. Why were you looking at me? I didn't know what to respond, and the girl on the beach was waiting for me to say something. There was no sign of the butterfly. And you, why were *you* looking at me? I sat down and she sat beside me. She held her hand in front of her face and peeked at me through her fingers. And she said: You don't look at someone the way you looked at me this morning unless what you are seeing pleases you more than all else. You have made me yours. I followed you here and from now on I will follow you always . . . I have nothing to latch on to. I have only you. I felt revulsion. Revulsion at the idea of losing myself in that voice, of ending up being devoured by a girl's voice in the midst of that expanse of sea and evening. The frothy waves surged higher. She said the sea frightened her, her whole life had been filled with fear: fear of night, of the moon that made her want to scream as soon as she saw it. Clouds terrified her, lightning sent her hiding under the bed. Later she grew scared of people: tall men, fat women, loud children, old people groping their way along because their eyes had died, barking dogs, birds launching themselves against the wind. Fear. Fear of everything. Fear of moving, dreaming, laughing. Fear that people might see what she was made of inside. Fear of a shout, a scolding, footsteps beneath her window, a piece of furniture that weeps in the quiet of the night. Fear of the dead who creep up on you and snatch the bedsheets. You see? Fear of these waves. But with you by my side I'm not afraid of anything. I listened to her without wanting to. I wished to walk the world alone. I should have stood up and run away. And I defended myself as best I could. I saw Eva riding a white horse where the sea met the distant sky. Eva who wanted nothing and asked for nothing. I will be whatever you want me to be; I will do whatever you want me to do. We will have a little house with a pot of parsley in the kitchen window. A vegetable garden full of turnips and carrots, cabbages and chicory. A cage with rabbits, a henhouse with six hens and six geese running about more vigilant than a watchdog. I will cook you lunch and dinner. You will have your fill of roast chicken, grilled rabbit, soup with monkfish and crabmeat and megrim and mussels . . . marmalades made from purple and amber plums, apricots, strawberries, cherries. You will have apple-scented sheets, rain-scented towels, blankets like flakes of fog. What are you thinking? She ran a finger across my cheek. I looked away in anger. She stepped back and I turned and faced her. I love a girl who wants nothing, she wants nothing, she wants only to belong to herself, herself alone. She loves rivers that carry stars, she hangs them up and takes them down, she speaks to them, knows what they are made of. She loves rocks and fire. She is not afraid of anything. Not even of the dead she sends down the river by shoving them with her pitchfork. She needs no one. The girl without a fiancé ran a finger across my cheek. What are you thinking? Her name is Eva and she is the most beautiful girl in the world. Stop, stop! She rides her horse alone. Brave. And lowering my voice I added: So what if I looked at you? She rose and walked a few steps toward the sea, stood there for a moment and then came back. She leaned down, her hair spilling over me, and I heard her voice, almost a whisper in my ear. Remember. My name is Isabel. And she headed toward the waves and strode into the water, deeper and deeper. I never saw her again.

XIX

What I Should Have Said

I SHOULD HAVE SHAKEN HER, GIVEN HER A GOOD SHAKE AS I shouted idiot, you idiot, why such desire to die when you have your whole life ahead of you? We lead our lives, all of us, without knowing what awaits us, but the more time you have before you, the greater the hope. It is a fresh life that turns the corner of every new year, and the year that commences might be one of cream or of honey, and then it ends, and the next one is different. I've known this since I was a boy: after sorrow, joy. I should have urged her to try to remember the world as it was in the beginning, when none of us knew we had bones, or what they were meant for, or what a worm was for, or the eagle that flies, or the leaf that detaches from the branch unweeping, unlike a human being would if he should fall like that, because the leaf knows, it carries this knowledge in its leaf-blood, that in the spring it will again be a leaf; its spirit will have slipped through the roots of the tree and up the trunk until it again breathes the winds of the rose. Rose under the sun, the rose will again become a rose. Believe me, I know better than anyone: rose when the dew . . . No, when the morning light on the dew . . . No, when the dew born of the damp night still . . . No, when the dew on leaves of grass still . . . To want to know the logic of death, whose purpose is to remove people from this world . . . there are too many of them. Out, out, out with you. Do not weep, do not wish to die. I was not made for the things you yearn for.

I was meant to roam the world. Do not search for death, He will come to you. A good whipping! That's what I should have given you instead of listening to you babble. You who had all the time in the world to keep Death waiting, with the joy of living, with the taste of apples and pears, of pomegranates with their queenly royal crown that appears when their curly leaves fall and the crown emerges sealing the hard green round box filled with diamonds as red as the blood when you cut yourself and a drop of fire appears like a pomegranate kernel with its wooden seed the color of your lips, not the seed, but the leaves of the flower pursued by the winds so that the tender crown may flaunt itself. That is how it should be: flaunt your tender crown, you who wanted to give your life to the water, a yellow butterfly in your hair. And when you marched into the waves, I should have grabbed you and dragged you to the sand and thrashed you till you were numb, and when you recovered you would no longer have wished to die, for it is true that a good thrashing expunges much sorrow. Do you hear me? I'm mad with rage because you have forced me to think about you and feel the weight of guilt for a death that you alone have chosen. I was at peace and you have thrust upon me the affliction of madness. Isabel.

Lying facedown, arms crossed, head resting on my arms, that person in front of me—that *I* that was and was not me—moaned: Go home. Mother and I are in the midst of planting cuttings of white carnations for First Communion bouquets and children's funerals. And with a small thread of a voice that mocked me, she cried, my name is Isabel.

XX

The Woman with the Canary

I WOULD HAVE WEPT HAD I NOT HEARD THE RINGING OF A LITTLE
bell approaching. Had I not glimpsed that moving light among
the pine trees, coming from the same direction as the sound of the
bell. Not until I had her in front of me did I see that it was an
old woman carrying a lantern. She stood there, dressed in black,
a black scarf around her head. She was holding the lantern, which
she placed on the ground, and an umbrella. Hiding behind her was
a little boy with a birdcage, a little bell inside it. Are you wounded?
asked the old woman. No. She had the same face as my godmother
Antònia: a long, lumpy nose, small, calm eyes, a mouth like a slit
made by a knife. I hadn't thought of her for many years because she
had died a long time ago. I could picture her seated on the bench in
the entranceway, watching me make mud pies, occasionally saying
to my mother, poor thing, with no husband. I pictured her doing
the laundry, tucking me in at night, all gentleness and sweet words
as she explained to me that feathery animals were angels disguised
as woodcocks or partridges, but they had to be killed like pigeons
in order for us to eat them and, with every bite, become winged
angels, and she would wave her hand up and down—onward,
onward—like the flapping of wings. When we can, the girls in
the village and I go to the castle to care for the wounded, the old
woman said. The little boy set the cage down beside the lantern,
it's a canary, he said. It was green, it jumped from perch to perch,

and with each jump the little bell rang. The bell keeps him happy and helps him sing. I'm surprised you're not wounded; all the boys and men I come across who are lost like you have some wound or other. The ones who are in the worst shape are taken to the castle. The old woman had such a hoarse voice that it troubled me. If you were wounded I would send someone for you and have you taken to the castle. I was on the point of yelling that, no, I was not wounded. Did you know there is a poor man at the castle who is coming to his end? He used to have seven canaries. Of the seven only one sang. If only I could hear it, he said when I told him I had a green canary. I promised him I would take it to him today, and I am; but it might be too late. Dead. Most of them die in the early morning. If only I could hear your canary, Senyora Isabel—my name is Isabel—I could believe that mine had not died in that terrible bombing, buried beneath the rubble while I was down at the docks, unloading. She paused and held the lantern closer to me. You can't fool me. You're ill. Your face is paler than cream and your eyes red from weeping. I have never wept, I told her, not even when I was little. Something inside me always grabbed hold of my tears and wouldn't let them out. If you don't need me, she said, I'll be on my way to the castle. The first thing I'll do is go see the baron, who went batty when his brother died with his knees shattered by blows from a rifle butt. He keeps himself locked in the flag room. She picked up the lantern and the umbrella from the ground. The little boy took the cage and dragged it along. As soon as they left it started to rain. And through the turbulence of the waves I could hear the little bell ringing.

XXI

A House by the Sea

I COULD ALREADY SEE THE LIGHTS OF A VILLAGE WHEN I NOTICED an isolated house with its second-floor balcony all lit up. Drenched, seeking a place to shelter more than anything else, I entered the garden by jumping over the low wall that enclosed it. I found refuge beneath the balcony, but the wind was driving the torrential rain against me; I searched and searched until I found an unlocked door. The smell did not lie: I had entered the kitchen. I groped around and came across a hanging bag from which I extracted a piece of bread. If I could only find the salt and the cruet of olive oil . . . My mouth was beginning to water, while outside the lighting and thunder and clamoring sea locked in a fierce tempest. Footsteps coming from the garden suddenly transformed into a silhouette in the doorway; the door swung inward against me as the shadow reached in to switch on the light. How I wished the ground could have swallowed me up. A man in a trench coat dripping with water—he was clearly the owner—stood there calmly looking at me. Without a word he opened a small cupboard and brought out a plate of sliced ham. If you're hungry, eat. I see you've found the bread. My hunger vanished on the spot. He was neither old nor young, ageless almost. He had a high forehead—it seemed to never end—and cheeks covered with dry, dead skin. His perfectly aligned teeth were green. The look he gave me seemed to come from deep within; it was as if he were returning from another world, and encountering the real world pained him. He had a gold clover pinned to his tie. I gave him the same story: the soldiers, the war, losing my way. You certainly look lost. He said I could spend the night. There's an extra room upstairs. He helped me light a fire. The rain buffeted the roof, claps of thunder crawled in the distance; yet the storm was fleeing. I lay down on the floor with the bedspread for a mattress. I wanted to be near the hearth. My clothes were drying on the back of a chair. I could hear water dripping on the tin roof. The crackling of the fire lulled me to sleep. I was enveloped by a sense of peace that cannot be explained . . . By the low wall over which I had jumped, a boy who looked like me was blowing soap bubbles with a cane that he periodically dipped in a tin can; the bubbles hovered above a drowned girl whose body was being swept in and out by the waves. A hazy figure clutched at the bubbles that did not burst and tossed them into the air as if they were oranges, mumbling something about a vegetable patch with turnips and carrots. Many of the bubbles turned into human heads that floated upward gazing at the sky. They surged and sank with the breathing of the sea. Death, with green teeth, sat on the belly of a cloud. Seven women with feet of gold huddled together blowing seven long trumpets that spewed bubbles into the sea, while Death's scythe awaited the order to begin reaping the floating heads . . . I awoke drenched in sweat. A woman's husky voice on the other side of the door was calling me to come down to breakfast.

～〜

Senyora Isabel, the woman with the canary, was standing by the table waiting for me. She recognized me immediately. I ate breakfast alone and then, not knowing what else to do, I stepped outside and began clearing weeds and briers. At lunch time, the Senyor of the house by the sea knocked on the window and signaled for me to come in. A blue and white gingham tablecloth covered the table, the crockery was white, the goblets of thick glass. What's your name? As he unfolded his napkin, the man of the house by the sea asked me to stay for the week.

———≺———

At night we ate in the kitchen. Senyora Isabel prepared the food for us ahead of time and sometimes we didn't even need to heat it up. With the last bite still in our mouths we would head out for a walk. You forgot to turn off the balcony light. Leaving it on, he said, always makes me want to come home. We would sit on a rock and look at the sea. We returned as the bell in the village tower chimed at midnight, a sound that struck me as strange, for I had not heard it since the war began. We hardly spoke. One evening just as we sat down to dinner, the man of the house by the sea, circling his hand above his head, said: We are all organized energy. The entire universe is energy. Not knowing what to say, I looked away.

He showed me around. The house was large, but I won't say much about the place because he talks about it at length in the papers he left. But I will speak of the foyer that was rather long and not very wide. On the right-hand wall, coming from the dining room, hung a coat rack with a stool on either side. In front of the coat rack was a mirror that reached almost from the floor to the ceiling; its black frame of burnished wood had a garland of roses, the largest of which was at the top, right in the middle.

Scattered among the open roses were little buds, with many carefully arranged leaves around them that someone had painted green and time had partially stripped of color.

XXII

A RED LIGHT

SITTING, AS ALWAYS, FACING THE SEA, WE SAW A RED LIGHT BLINK-
ing in the distance, on the village side. Shadows were stirring on
the beach not far from where we sat; they were talking, but we
could not hear what they said. We noticed right away that they
were dragging a rowboat toward the water. While they were still
close to shore they began to flash a red light at the red light that
was signaling to them from a distance. Not ten minutes had elapsed
since the rowboat had headed out to sea when we heard an airplane
engine. Both the light in the bay and the distant red light stopped
signaling each other. Flares leapt from a large ship into the sky,
streaks of fire searching for the airplane. It all ended with several
explosions, followed by tongues of fire that licked the sky. The rowboat did not return and the sound of the plane faded away. A spot
blazed in the middle of the sea. The bells announced midnight.
Shall we go? Yes, let's.

When we reached the house Senyor led me to the foyer. He stopped
in front of the mirror and asked me more than once if I saw anything in it. I found it hard to fall asleep that night. Several times I
heard him going up and down the stairs. What did he see in that

cloudy mirror that was as old as the one on my mother's wardrobe, which as a young boy I used to press against until I had no nose? One night I made an effort not to fall asleep so I could learn what transpired during Senyor's frequent trips up and down the stairs. I put my eye to the keyhole. The light in his bedroom was on: I could see the reflection on the dining room floor. He walked by, coughing, and suddenly came over to my door. I jumped into bed. All at once I wanted out of that house, but there was something about the look in the man's eyes—so often filled with unease, so often appearing to beg for mercy—that made me stay. I felt sorry for him.

I had grown tired of the apprehension I experienced every night as we sat in front of the sea waiting for the stroke of midnight. And of the fear I felt on the occasions—and there had been many—when I stood before the mystery of that mirror. And I, who had always carried the religious medallions in my pocket, all dirty and crumpled, now hung them around my neck. Old Isabel also wore some, although the modesty of her dresses meant that I never saw them. But I had caught a glimpse of a black cord like the one around my neck.

———

Until finally one morning, Senyora Isabel pounded on my door around the time she usually arrived for work. Senyor was lying on the floor in the middle of the foyer with his eyes open, stiff as a board. He was still alive. We struggled to carry him upstairs and get him into bed. Old Isabel asked if she should send for the doctor who lived in a village some ways away. His pleading eyes went back and forth between us. I don't want a doctor, Adrià.

It was the first time he had called me by my name; he always summoned me with a mere come here, help me, sit down, come upstairs, follow me. And it struck me that perhaps because he uttered it with the voice of a sick person, my name sounded different, it aged me and made me feel stronger. That man trusted me. He stayed in bed for days. I took his meals and bowls of herbal tea up to him. I changed his clothes, I washed him, shaved him, kept him company at night, sitting by the balcony. Don't leave me . . . I drew nearer. Don't leave me.

⤙

One night when he had fallen asleep and was breathing calmly, I went into the foyer. I stood under the bulb that cast a yellow light and studied my reflection in the mirror, which was as old and cloudy as always. In it I saw myself, part of the coat rack, a stool . . . I looked at my feet, my legs, my hands at the end of my arms, my chest, neck, cheeks, eyes. My whole person. What did the man of the house by the sea see in the mirror?

Some nights, if he was resting peacefully, I would go into the library and, after gazing at the sea from the balcony, I would take a book. But I could never make much sense of what I read and soon tired of it. One night I braved going out after the chimes had sounded midnight. A light rain was falling, and the scent of the sea was intoxicating. The sand shifted under my feet, mist covered the water and lowered the sky. I walked on and on until I reached the dead, deserted village. I saw a light in a window near a ravine, and as I drew closer I tripped on a pile of stones and bricks. I climbed on the stones and peered into a room with a bed covered by a red quilt and a Virgin Mary with a crown of roses hanging above the headboard. A girl was undressing. She slipped her nightgown over her head, pulled her underskirt down to her feet and stepped out. I couldn't see very well because the curtains, though translucent, blurred her image. I would have liked to meet her, talk to her, know what she was thinking. Sleep by her side.

When I returned to the house by the sea and was about to climb the stairs I saw a light in the foyer. Wrapped in a robe, Senyor was sitting on a stool in front of the mirror. He did not see me.

He died the following day as evening was setting in. He had had a peaceful night. When he woke his eyes no longer had the frightened look they had on other occasions, but his face was devoid of color. He removed an envelope from beneath the pillow and asked me to keep it. I'm leaving, he said, I won't be here long . . . you'll find my will in the envelope. My last will and testament. Open it as soon as I'm gone. He ate nothing. When Senyora Isabel saw that I was returning the food tray untouched, she mumbled that it was as if he were dead already. I kept vigil by his bedside all night, as one might for a saint. Little by little his skin wizened in a disturbing fashion. His eyes, fixed on the ceiling, sank farther into the sockets. He had not yet reached true old age, but in a matter of hours all of him changed into a bag of bones that was slowly shriveling up. It was as if there were a child in the bed. The palm of his right hand was turned upward, displaying a bleeding wound, long and narrow.

It fell to me to bury him. Aided by some kindly soul, the rector of the parish had fled the village at the beginning of the revolution. The gravedigger had gone to live with a sister who was as ancient as he was. The church had been emptied of saints, and an old farmer who had been an altar boy as a child had taken it upon himself to ring the hours. Children played in the streets with the candelabras that had stood on the high altar, a gift from the masters of the house where old Isabel had served, people, who like so many others, had died with their faces to the wall.

I dug a pit in the corner of the cemetery, after first removing quite a bit of dogwood. Five spans beneath the earth, bones began to appear; I picked one up as one would a branch. It was blackened and decayed; whether it had belonged to an arm or a leg I could not say. A young boy was watching and asked if he could have it. Will you give it to me? He took it and ran away jumping and shouting, it's from a dead person! I have the bone of a dead person! The man who brought us wood, having been notified by Senyora Isabel, helped me carry the proprietor of the house by the sea to the cemetery and lower him into the earth. On top we placed a few stones that we took from the pile beneath the window of the girl I saw undressing for bed.

That night, after Senyora Isabel had left, I opened the envelope. Inside was a thick sheet of paper and, in a clear handwriting, the words: "I bequeath all my possessions, furniture and property to Adrià Guinart, who has kept me company until the hour of my death. In exchange I ask one last favor of him: that he shred and burn all my documents. Pere Ardèvol." Seated at the desk in the library, I began to peruse his papers. There were many, all of them carefully classified in faded folders. Letters to a bank in Barcelona, letters to the village mayor discussing some land Senyor Ardèvol wanted to sell. Letters from a friend, Esteve Aran, dated in Arenys de Mar, in which the friend spoke of the mystery of dreams and the memories of another life. In the last of these letters the friend announced that he would soon be paying Senyor a visit. In a file bound with greater care than the rest was a group of papers that spoke only of mirrors. Senyor Ardèvol stated at the beginning of these that each person is the mirror of the entire universe. Of God. And then I came across some sheets of paper—written in a handwriting that was difficult to make out—that explained how he had come to that house and told the story of the mirror in the foyer. The new day found me still reading.

PART
TWO

XXIII

THE INHERITANCE

IN HIS PAPERS, SENYOR ARDÈVOL EXPLAINED THAT HE HAD RE-
ceived an inheritance from his uncle at the age of twenty-two. He
was orphaned when he was very young and didn't remember a
thing about his parents. They had both died at the same time, and
the circumstances of their death had remained a mystery, at least to
him. Nobody had ever told him how or when those who put him
on this earth had passed away.

On one occasion, in a chest of drawers at his uncle's apartment,
he had come across a portrait of a beautiful woman with light-colored hair and eyes. It was summer, and the discovery of that portrait would be forever fused in his memory with the smell of wilted
flowers and afternoons that seemed to never end. Years later, as
a way of shoring himself up when depression struck, he would
remember that photograph, hoping it was of his mother. Trying to
feel the warm caress of those hands on his forehead, cleansing him
of whatever bad he carried within him.

He had had little contact with his Uncle Hipòlit. He was an ami-
able man, who spent his life calling on others, always arriving with
tins of bonbons or boxes of pastries for the ladies, always keen to
play cards with their husbands. But he never received anyone in his
own home. He lived alone in Barcelona, in an apartment on Carrer
Aragó that was richly appointed with fine old furniture, authentic
rugs, thick wooden doors, and stained glass windows. His uncle's

fortune consisted of a house in a coastal village, many hectares of land and a more than respectable amount of securities—a term I was not familiar with but I assumed referred to some sort of valuable documents. In his younger years, Senyor Ardèvol had lived with his nanny, a country woman who was worth more than her weight in gold. She had instilled in him the notion that growing wheat was the most important endeavor in the world, and that a well-formed cabbage was of greater merit than a gentleman in patent-leather shoes and a satin-trimmed jacket. As soon as he was old enough, his uncle locked him away in a boarding school. All that had once been skies and open fields, freshwater springs and chirping birds, was replaced by walls with peeling paint and high windows with foggy panes. Expelled for bad behavior, he bounced from one school to the next. When it came time to choose a career, after much thought, he decided on architecture. His uncle then lodged him in a family-run pension uptown. Each month, to cover his expenses, he sent him a sum of money that was neither too substantial nor too paltry. He spent Christmas and his uncle's Saint's Day at the apartment on Carrer Aragó. In his papers, Senyor Ardèvol described his uncle as a quiet man, with nervous eyes, droopy eyebrows, a prominent jaw and a short neck, a man of few words, orderly and well-mannered. But then one year the customary Christmas invitation never arrived. He didn't dare show up unannounced at his uncle's apartment, and instead waited for an explanation for the unusual conduct. A few weeks later he received a letter from a notary informing him that his uncle had died of heart failure and had left him all of his possessions. Senyor Ardèvol said he quit his studies as though removing a tether from around his neck.

People bored him, and the few friends he had finally tired of him too. They would say: Your mind always seems elsewhere. He had maintained only one friendship, that of Esteve Aran, a man engrossed in the study of the mystery of existence, who was jealous of his knowledge and rarely made any reference to it. The bond between them was so strong that they could almost guess each other's thoughts. The furniture in Carrer Aragó ended up at Els Encants flea market or in antiques shops: Everything was scattered. Senyor Ardèvol went to live in the house in the village, a place he had loved since his first visit there.

The façade gave onto a quiet road. In the back was a flowerless garden enclosed by a low wall with a door in the middle that was kept open and led to a field bordering a beach of fine sand and clear waters. The house had two floors. On one side was an abandoned vegetable garden, on the other, a derelict shed. On the ground floor, on either side of the foyer, were two rooms that faced the street: a sitting room and an office. At the end of the foyer, a glass door opened onto the dining room, to the right of which was the kitchen and, to the left, a storage room filled with firewood. A spiral staircase in the dining room led upstairs to a large parlor with book-lined walls. The room he had kept for himself was off that parlor. On the street side there were two other bedrooms, one reserved for his friend Aran to use during his visits, the other for storing odds and ends.

The furniture was black, the rugs red and worn in spots. The lights were curious: simple electrical wires that hung from the ceiling and ended in lightbulbs that cast a tenuous yellow glow. The very day after his arrival—he recounted—the doorbell rang while he was still asleep. He dressed in a hurry and rushed to the door sleepy-eyed. Before him stood an old woman who reminded him of his nanny. My name is Isabel. She informed him that his uncle had employed her to cook and clean for him whenever he came to stay. And if Senyor Ardèvol so wished, she would be pleased to serve him as well. She knew he was Senyor Arnau's nephew and that he had inherited everything; in other words, that he was the master now. He took her on. She arrived at nine in the morning, worked well and cooked well, and after lunch she washed the dishes and left.

Time passed quickly those first few weeks. Little by little he grew accustomed to acting the part of the idle property owner. After living for so long in family-run lodgings and pensions, the house seemed to him a palace. He asked the carpenter to build him more shelves to hold the books he had brought from Barcelona, old tomes with strange names: a book of advice on dealing with the devil, a book about the confessions of the saintliest saints. He moved into the house in mid-autumn. Seated at his desk on the second floor, he had a view of the sea, the choppy waters, the great surging waves.

On turning a page, I came upon a few brief notes explaining his difficulty in recalling a certain dream. Many details had slipped his mind, and others had appeared only to vanish again, all of it welling up from the deepest recesses of his spirit. Wishing to relive a dream is futile, Senyor Ardèvol wrote. He explained that he had never dreamed that he was blinded by the sun, never dreamed of colors, never heard any sounds or people talking or screaming . . . and yet on that particular night he had dreamed in vivid colors. He recalled a storm from which he had struggled to escape. The wind upturned leaves he could not see but whose suffering on the branches he could feel. Drops of water fell from every leaf as though the entire orchard were weeping, blinded by lightning, furiously shaken by the winds. But before he could retell that night's dream, which had left him riddled with anxiety, he said he first needed to discuss the issue of knives and the fear they had caused him as a child.

The mere sight of a knife forced him to close his eyes; it terrified him. There had been a boy, Fermí Baixeres, who was the best student in his class and had stirred many of his classmates' interest with the odd things he said and did. One morning during recess, near a grotto with a saint's shrine surrounded by hydrangeas, the boy had stood in the middle of a group of admirers and announced that he was going to cut his hand to the bone to show them how little he cared about physical pain. Fermí had greyish-blond hair and eyes so blue they seemed empty; the clique of boys who disliked him—there were those, too—had nicknamed him "symphony in grey." He was thin, with broad shoulders and arms that were too long for his body. He had once said in jest that he was clearly descended from the chimpanzee. It was a kitchen knife with a thick handle and a thin, sharp blade. Concentrating, the tip of his tongue between his teeth, Fermí traced a line that started from his palm and ended at the base of his little finger. Over and over he ran the knife along the line, till gouts of blood welled forth. The boys watching him held their breath. And perhaps he would have accomplished what he set out to do, which was to cut deeper until he hit the bone, had he not first collapsed to the ground like a sack of potatoes.

There was no knife in that night's dream, but there was a dagger with an undulated blade, perforated with five holes. The following day Senyor Ardèvol had the same dream. This time, it was not a dagger but a sword. The first dream had begun with wind rustling the leaves under a sky of black clouds pierced by streaks of lightning. He had never known how to describe a tempest, much less one born of emptiness, one that filled him with forgotten sensations that wiped out everything in their wake, as if calmly tossing everything into a well to meld with time and color. In the dream he found himself walking through an unfamiliar village in a driving rain when he came upon a small square with houses on three sides, none more than two stories high, with tiled roofs. On the fourth side, atop a low wall with an iron railing, sat a grey cat with eyes like Fermí Baixeres's, looking at him, studying him. He did not know how he had arrived at the square. The rain stopped. Everything was soothing. Decorated with flowering plants, the windows seemed full of people whom he could not see but could feel watching his every move, as was the sitting cat. And suddenly he found he was dressed in a fashion typical of ages past, a loose-fitting frock that covered his shoulders and fell to his feet. Standing in the middle of the penumbral square, with the cat's eyes glimmering, the thick quietude clouded his senses. Had his perception failed him? The loose-fitting frock, which had appeared black, was in fact white with an embroidered cross in the center of the chest, like the frocks worn by the entourage that accompanied him. He was approaching a shadowy patch. From it slowly emerged a figure, also dressed in white, also bearing a cross in the middle of the chest, with arms wrapped in chain mail, as were all the men's arms, including his own. When they were abreast of each other, the figure extended an arm. His hand held a moon-colored sword with an iron hilt. The tip of the sword grazed his forehead and the flat of it came to rest first on one shoulder, then the other. And everything faded as if it were somehow being pulled from afar. Around him remained only the houses, the wall with the railing, and the cat staring at him. At that moment he sensed a presence behind him. He wanted to turn around but could not, he felt a dagger sinking into his back. A puddle of blood formed at his feet and he collapsed.

The dreams had shaken Senyor Ardèvol so much that he had to flee. He rushed to Arenys de Mar to visit Aran. He told his friend that he needed to take a long trip; his mental health was at stake, but the idea of embarking on a trip alone made him anxious. Aran had smiled, poured him a large glass of cognac, and confessed that he had had a longstanding interest in Gothic cathedrals and had wanted to visit Chartres for some time. His friend's need for a trip was the enticement he sought for his own journey.

—⤜—

The two men arrived in the village where they had resolved to spend the night. Everything Senyor Ardèvol saw, the streets along which he walked, the houses on either side of the streets, the portals, the balconies, everything, *everything*, seemed strangely familiar. He did not mention any of this to his friend, but Aran must have sensed that something was troubling him because he asked him several times if he was unwell. Senyor Ardèvol responded that the journey by car had fatigued him, but that a good night's sleep should restore him. He had a light dinner and fell asleep shortly after retiring. The sheets had a pleasant smell of old-fashioned wash—lavender, he thought—and the pillow and the thick duvet were stuffed with feathers. He awoke with a start, the night still pitch black. And however much he tried he could not fall asleep again. He was inclined to rise, but what would he do then? And even as he was telling himself that he would not get up, he jumped out of bed and dressed. The streets were deserted. There was not a soul in sight. From a market came the stench of rotting vegetables and stale meat. From atop a belfry, the bell tolled; it was four o'clock. He thought of Henry IV, whose name he had seen engraved on the tower of some palace. An urge that came from deep within prompted him to enter the village square: It was the one in his dream. On three of its sides stood two-story houses with tiled roofs and flowers in the windows. Atop a low wall with a railing, a grey cat stared at him. He planted himself in front of it, but the cat did not move or avert its gaze. Its eyes were fixed on his, and it was he who had to turn his head to escape them. A tempest of thoughts left him paralyzed in the center of the square. He felt as though a steel blade were being driven into his back. He wiped the sweat from his brow . . . Toward the east, a tender light heralded the day. His head was spinning as he left the square. The cat was still perched on the low wall. The sky was already pink when he entered the hotel.

XXIV

THE MIRROR IN THE FOYER

SENYOR ARDÈVOL COULD NOT RECALL WHEN HE HAD STARTED going out at night. At first he had not ventured beyond the beach, though later he went as far as the village, at an hour when everyone was asleep. Three streets flowed into the church square, the middle one continuing on to the outskirts of the village. Past midnight on one of those many nights, he stopped in front of a window with a light on inside. Standing on a pile of stones, he spotted a girl undressing. He could not see her clearly because the window had curtains which, although sheer, clouded the view of the girl's face. He liked that vaporous image. She probably had the broad face of a peasant girl, perhaps snub-nosed, healthy, with dreamy eyes, but he imagined a creamy blend of white and pink, eyes that offered a glimpse of the soul, trembling lips . . . a girl who came to life against a backlight, so that he might contemplate her without really seeing her, and thus be free to reflect on her remembered image to the point of obsession.

━⤚

Senyor Ardèvol returned from the trip with his friend Aran more anguished than ever and stayed indoors for several weeks. Until, little by little, he resumed his former routine.

It had all begun one night when the sea was in a swell of fury. He was in such a hurry to return home before the rain came that he started running and arrived at his kitchen door with his heart pounding. As he was stepping inside, a bolt of lightning fretted a thread across the sky. His heart still fatigued, he was making his way to the foyer to hang up his trench coat when he felt as though something were trying to stop him. He could not make sense of it, but it seemed that his legs would not respond and that his heart, so agitated only a moment before, had stopped for the space of a few seconds. It wasn't exactly that; it was more as though a mysterious force were emptying him of his "I." That was all. When he finally found himself in the parlor, he downed half a bottle of cognac and, although it was late, he read for a while. He chose a book at random and opened it to the beginning of a page that argued, roughly, that man is the master of his actions, free to desire or not to desire, by the power of his thinking and the virtue of his reason; imagination, it said, turns perilous when we ponder the act of becoming and the conditions that govern it. As I read Senyor Ardèvol's account of the book, I could not quite grasp the meaning of this. The book stated, and I read it many times over so I would remember it . . . or, rather, it didn't so much state as pose the question: Under what conditions can one become another?

On the night following the events just described it was bitterly cold outside and he had to bundle up. He left the house through the kitchen door, leaving it unlocked. The fields were covered in frost. He sat on a rock facing the sea. Senyor Ardèvol explained that he had never had a meditative disposition, but that he was a contemplative man. Enamored of the mystery of life, he had never felt the need, as his friend Aran had, of attempting to decipher it. He considered it an unassailable mystery. And a mystery must struggle—that is its principal reason for being—so that its great beauty will not be stripped from it. The sea resembled a lake that night. Small waves died on the sand, flat, with a litany of sighs. Suddenly the girl in the window came to mind, a faraway thought lost in time. Why had his interest waned, when so many times before she had been the enticement to go into the village? And he began to think of death. Senyor Ardèvol wrote that when people die they should remain frozen in that moment, like those human shapes that have been perfectly preserved in a vacuum and turn to dust with the slightest puff of air. They should die with their senses fully alive, in the middle of the street while strolling through a sleepy village.

The moon deposited slivers of light on his balcony window. Smudges of brightness that elongated and widened in a dance, phantoms of stripes, shiny blocks, darkened spaces. When he returned, he stopped in the foyer and, while hanging up his coat, was overcome by a powerful urgency to turn around. In front of him hung the mirror. Senyor Ardèvol described it. Beveled. Mottled. A mahogany frame with a garland of flowers and leaves. He had never felt the need to look at himself in the mirror, other than when he shaved or was at the tailor's trying something on. But that night he looked at himself for a while, as if bewitched, not by his own image but by something within the mirror. His features, he wrote, were not harmonious: his brow too high, his cheeks too sunken, his eyes too small. In the mirror, slightly to the right, appeared a pair of eyes with a disquieting fixity, like those of the cat in the square. Only larger, closer together, the whites of the eye more generous. Questioning eyes. He felt—and the thought anguished him more than anything else—that those were his own eyes, though they were not. Those eyes wanted to convey things he could not understand. With great effort, for the fascination was intense, he looked away and, when his eyes returned to the mirror, there was nothing there. Only, as always, part of the coat rack, the lightbulb that cast a yellow gleam, and his own image. He went to the living room and lit a fire; he needed the company of the flames. He was prepared to read until he fell asleep, so as not to think. But he found he could not read a line. An understandable curiosity compelled him to return to the foyer. The mirror was in its usual place, with its mottled specks and flowers. He tapped the lightbulb to see if the pendular movement would summon a reflection into the mirror. He wanted to see those eyes again.

⤙

While he was having dinner he vaguely pondered the last page he had read. *To receive in oneself the other's form without his substance.* Later, as he sat facing the sea, he was again consumed by anguish. He soon rose and made his way back, stopping for a while to observe the house from the low wall. He entered and immediately approached the mirror and planted himself squarely before it. After waiting for a few minutes that seemed interminable, he began to perceive those eyes. They came forth slowly, questioning and sad, not on the right side of the mirror as they had the first time, but centered on his own eyes, those eyes that should have been his but were another's. A smudge, milky at first, then slowly becoming clearer, began to acquire the contours of a shape which he soon recognized as an arm covered with chain mail, at the end of which was a hand with long fingers like his own, the palm open, a wound in the center. Some letters began to form to the side of the arm: Stigmata. He turned his back to the mirror. When he wanted to turn around again, he found that he could not. Until the bell tower in the village struck one o'clock. He then looked in the mirror and found the usual mollifying objects: part of the coat rack, the lightbulb, and himself. Stigmata. Where had that word come from? He had never used it. In his adolescence there had been that knife wound on Baixeres's hand . . . He looked up the meaning of the word. Stigmata: Mark or brand, particularly one made with a hot iron as a sign of infamy or, possibly, slavery. Senyor Ardèvol wrote that a saint—Augustine—had helped him take his mind off the mirror. "I had sunk far away from Thine eyes. In Thine eyes, there was nothing more repugnant than I."

He looked out onto the garden from the railing at the kitchen window. The moon was golden. He had chosen a book from the library, which he now started to read while making himself a pot of coffee. One of the characters in the book—he couldn't recall which—had said that those who allow their souls to be populated by terror see things that do not exist. Senyor Ardèvol wrote that he had laughed so hard he had almost choked. He had allowed himself to be frightened by the mottled mirror and by those eyes as he might have been by a lion or giraffe-shaped cloud munching on the blueness of the sky. With the book under his arm and the coffee pot filled to the brim, he marched up to the mirror and stood before it, defiant. His own true self and nothing other than that was what he saw in the mirror, and poorly reflected at that: the right side on the left, the left on the right. He had bid farewell forever to those eyes, to whatever he had been able to glimpse in that mirror. He went upstairs feeling as though he had just been released from prison after years of confinement. He took another book, an essay about Saint Thomas. The human soul begins . . . I can't recall everything Senyor Ardèvol wrote . . . through the door . . . the embryo . . . The father does not create the soul . . . reading those papers, written in a handwriting that, more than read, had to be deciphered, it took me some time to understand that the embryo is the beginning of a person. The father creates the bones and the blood, the body. A soul desiring to live again in this world awaits the infant's first cry, then slips inside him . . . It wasn't altogether clear whether the soul entered at the child's first cry or when the child was still surrounded by water . . . Senyor Ardèvol put down the book and walked to the balcony. The moon glowed golden. Old preoccupations stirred within him: the wound on Baixeres's hand, the dream in which he had been stabbed with a dagger with a five-hole blade so the wound would stay open. It had been a while since the church bell had chimed midnight, that time of day when the hidden sun slows the flow of blood and turns sleeping men into creatures that invite death. Suddenly, as though ejected from his chair, he sprang up and headed to the foyer. He dragged one of the stools before the mirror and sat down. Motionless. He gazed into the mirror with a steady heart and not a trace of fear, and saw appearing within it those eyes that looked at him and he at them. And that night the face took shape. The face of someone who had suffered greatly. The lips were full, those of someone who had reaped life's pleasures. Despite the mouth, the face conveyed a deep asceticism that is only attained over the course of an intensely-lived existence. On the bottom edge of the mirror something gleamed that he could not quite recognize . . . Here the writing ended.

I went to the cemetery and stayed there a while. As I was returning home along the road, I spotted a bicycle propped against the front door and, standing next to it, a man. He immediately told me his name: Esteve Aran. He explained that, on his way from Arenys, when he was halfway here, a checkpoint patrol had confiscated his car and given him a bicycle by way of compensation. I led him into the house and explained everything that had happened. I spoke about my affection for his friend and, as I had not yet destroyed the papers, I allowed him to read them. The following day I showed him the will and told him I did not wish to keep anything for myself. I already had a house; I wanted to give everything to Senyora Isabel, who was old and poor. He listened, had me write down my wishes and assured me that he would make certain everything was taken care of. Shortly after his departure I, too, left, having first handed a weeping Senyora Isabel the key to the house. She produced a tiny box from her apron pocket: Look inside. Pinned to a piece of cork slept a yellow butterfly with spread wings. As soon as I recovered from the surprise, I asked her who had given it to her. One of the girls who sometimes helps me at night at the castle. She knows you. What is her name, what is she like? She knows you, she has long hair, very long . . . she's a good girl. Her name is Isabel, like mine.

XXV

I Returned

I HAD ONLY BEEN WALKING FOR A SHORT WHILE WHEN I DECIDED to turn back. I stopped in front of the house: The balcony light was on, as it had been before. The door to the kitchen was unlocked, as before. I stood in the middle of the kitchen and called out a couple of times, Senyora Isabel, Senyora Isabel! There was no answer. I did not understand why I had returned. I inspected the entire house, from top to bottom. The ashes of the papers Senyor Aran and I had burned were still in the fireplace in the library. I took out the tiny box, which I had almost forgotten was in my pocket. I grasped the butterfly and caressed its wings with a finger, turning them to dust. I suddenly felt the desire to wait for dawn so I could return to the crab-infested rock, find Isabel and choke her. Why had she made me believe she wanted to kill herself? Was it worth it to see her again? What was it, in life, that was truly worthwhile? Everything I had experienced in that house had somehow shackled me, everything had the whiff of the man who had taken me in even though he had caught me stealing a piece of bread. Never again would I live in a house such as that by the sea, with the old man still locked inside with his fear. I saw the lightbulb reflected in the mirror. I tapped it so it would swing. Planted in front of the mirror was my own being: the dark shirt, the loose threads where a button had fallen off, the trousers that were a bit short . . . The light was swinging back and forth. I held my breath; in the mirror, something seemed to be struggling to emerge . . . I bounded up the stairs four steps at a time and jammed the backrest of a chair under the doorknob. Trucks full of men singing war tunes rolled by along the road. Lying on the tiles in front of the hearth, as I had that first night in the house, I finally managed to fall asleep. I awoke at daybreak. I went down the stairs slowly and, without thinking twice, I banged the stool against the mirror until it shattered.

XXVI

The Three Acacia Town

Anyone would have stopped to take in the view of that dark and dreary valley cleft by a river. Not far from a farmhouse, cows were pasturing serenely under a boy's watch. Soon both cows and boy started walking. Once they were inside the stable, I made my way down to the river, for I was parched. Beyond the farmhouse, perched atop the hill, was a town with a column of smoke billowing from its center. The smoke issued from a house, the finest in the main square. The second-floor balconies were spitting fire. Everyone was shouting. Women rushed from the portal carting chairs, armchairs, a blue and gold headboard, drawers, three bedside tables, a black rocking chair . . . A few old men and children watched the women as they busied themselves emptying the house. I heard a voice saying that if the flames on the ground floor were to emerge from the portal, they would burn the three acacias in the main square. Let everything burn! House and acacias! They aren't ours. Beside the fountain a man lay sprawled face-down, three crimson holes in his back. That's the master of the house that's on fire, an old man in a beret informed me, his wizened face scarcely larger than a fist. All this effort to amass a fortune and look at him now. If it were up to me, I'd toss him back inside so he would serve as kindling and nothing would be wasted.

The old man took me back to his place; he lived alone in a kind of den with recently whitewashed walls and a hearth as black as horror. He fed me and recounted the story of the owner of the burning house: He had arrived in the village as a young man, in search of work, any kind of work, and the wealthiest landowner hired him because he was as strong as an ox and not afraid of hard work. A couple of years later he married the heiress, Rosa, who had skinned knees from kneeling in constant prayer. She had always said she wanted to be a nun. Yet without intending to, the man who was a stranger to the village had frustrated her intentions: Rosa fell in love with him. The father opposed the union, but the girl did not relent until he acquiesced. The word immediately spread that she, who had turned away so many suitors, had been seduced by the drifter who had used his cunning to woo her. But the marriage grew cold. The father died, and all of the property passed into the drifter's hands. They had a daughter, Eulàlia, despised by her father, who had not wanted children. After a strange malady, Rosa followed her father to the cemetery. The drifter treated his daughter worse than a dog: His sole preoccupation was amassing wealth. No one was allowed a morsel of bread unless he unlocked the cupboard where it was kept. He cut thin slices and let them dry out. He was a nobody who had come into money, a parvenu. He was disliked, but people kept their heads down because they needed him. He did not allow water to be extracted from the well as needed: The rope would be worn thin. He borrowed other peoples' horses to conserve the horseshoes on his own. He let his teeth rot: Dentists were swindlers. All the fireplaces in his house had their chimneys capped to avoid the use of firewood; he believed that blocking the passage of air did more to heat the place than ruining forests by felling trees. He trimmed his fingernails with kitchen scissors because he had no others. When the barber cut his hair, he paid him with a few miserable pieces of fruit and the promise of more to come, though his trees were bare. Everyone despised him, yet anyone needing money was forced to go to him, though it was clear that the loan would come at a considerable price. Eulàlia had sad eyes and a body so frail she could barely stand. The entire village cried Miracle! Miracle! when she married the eldest son of a neighbor who had discovered her wandering lost in the forest one day, sobbing, saying she was running away. As she walked down the aisle she had the pallor of death. Her father, who did not accompany her that day, cursed her, for he would now be forced to hire someone to run the household. An old woman weighed down by many years and hardships came to serve in his home.

From time to time, he traveled to Barcelona, taking with him a small suitcase that appeared light when he left and heavy upon his return. The villagers all said that he had gone to buy gold. The miser's house was derelict, yet in people's minds it was covered with gold. When things finally came to a head, a few young men—the most impetuous in the village—having heard their parents lambasting the miser, broke into his house, seized him, and locked him up. Tiring of their inability to force him to divulge the location of his hidden treasure, they dragged him into the square, placed a paper hat on him and gave him a beating, while the old woman in his service and two neighbors set fire to the house. But first, they inspected the place from top to bottom, every nook and cranny, every crack in the wall. They axed closets, knocked down hollow-sounding walls, emptied wineskins, drove holes into the chimneys . . . But the gold did not appear. It was decided that the old men of the village, with the help of the women and children, would dig up the miser's lands and search the crevices in every rock . . . and whoever found the gold would announce the news and it would be divided among them.

At nightfall there were still people in the street. Amid cries, laughter, and insults they threw debris on the miser who had arrived in the village as a young man. At dawn the house was a furnace. The leaves on the acacias were charred and would never grow again. The man in the beret and I moved closer to observe the dead man. Beneath the pile of garbage, only his feet showed.

XXVII

THE CAT MAN

I CROSSED THE ESPLANADE. A FIG TREE STOOD IN FRONT OF THE door to the café. Inside, everything was a jumble of broken glass. I sat down at a table to think, but I had no time to reflect on things because almost immediately a man with hunched shoulders and a limp entered. He was carrying a straw basket from which he produced a bottle of wine and half a baguette stuffed with bacon. He looked at me, waiting for someone? As you can see, life has come to a halt here. Did you follow the road or did you come through the village? I came by way of the road. So you haven't seen all the ashes in the street. There's not a dog left to wag its tail. Shrugging my shoulders, I said I didn't care if life had come to a stop and I wasn't waiting for anyone. He took a bite of his bread and a piece of bacon came out, just like the piece of ham had slipped out of the lethargic man's sandwich that day on the beach. You should remember to work hard, while you're young. Hand me a knife: second drawer on the right, under the countertop. I should have given him the knife and left; I wasn't in the mood for idle talk, but I liked sitting in the café, with the profusion of broken bottles and empty shelves, watching the flies buzzing about. The man with the straw basket was drinking wine straight from the bottle, his eyes closed, one hand under his chin to avoid staining his shirt.

He said it was his café, not by ownership but because he had frequented it for as long as he could remember, his entire life. He earned his keep by neutering cats and rendering small services. When the owner of the café was killed . . . sad, huh? Distant relatives had ordered the killing after demanding one hundred thousand pesetas from the owner and being told he didn't have it, which was the truth. But they thought he was simply refusing to pay up, and when things got heated, out came the rifles. That said, this café has always been mine and always will be, because I have nowhere else to go. Half the ceiling of my house has caved in. He paused for a moment as he looked at me, head lowered, eyes raised. Want to see the cat? I glanced outside, trying to appear distracted. I realize I'm rather dull. Unlike my father . . . he made earthenware jugs and bowls. When he touched the clay, an object came to life. As he talked, the man with the straw basket kept looking at me and sniggering as though he thought me some pipsqueak who had just flown the nest, so I told him that his father was not his father. He grasped the bottle and nearly smashed it on my head, but managed to reign himself in. His father, I explained, had only made his body; his soul was a lost soul that had searched for a home for years and had slipped inside his body when he had taken his first breath. With eyes full of rage, he asked me if I had been drinking from the fountain of the moon-pulled water. To shut me up, or so I believe, he removed a package from his basket. Want to see it? It was a stuffed cat with its tail pinned to its body and its ears up. A tabby. My wife couldn't stand the sight of it and I always put it on her bedside table . . . That's what I'd like to do with a lot of people: Stuff them with straw so they would be still and quiet. Fill them full of straw. This cat—this very cat—had belonged to some neighbors. A fantastic ratter, it was. A regal cat. Its owner lavished it with all manner of attentions: It ate from a porcelain dish and slept on velvet. They were rich, these neighbors, and could afford to keep as many cats as they wished. Every night I would bury my head in the pillow, consumed with envy. And I learned taxidermy so I could make the cat my own. I tied a chicken head with a string and lured the cat to the house by dangling it in front of him. He crept warily into the garden—and then he was mine. I've slept with the cat next to me ever since. Even on my wedding night. When my wife died—may she rest in peace—I learned to meow, and before falling asleep, with the cat under the covers, I would meow for a while as if the cat were serenading me. And I still do. It helps me fall sleep.

XXVIII

PRIDE

THE DAY WAS BREAKING. I HAD SLEPT POORLY, MY ARMS ON THE table and my head resting on them. The back of my neck was sore and I had a taste of copper in my mouth. Beyond the fog-shrouded esplanade, shadowy figures were getting in and out of a van with its taillights on. Two men were coming toward the café, each with a box on his shoulders. As they were entering, two shots rang out. They've finished him off. The cat man woke up, his eyes filled with fear. It's nothing, grandpa, it's nothing. Just a salvo. The men started removing bottles of cognac from the boxes and stacking them on the counter.

Other men were approaching, speaking in loud voices. The last man to enter the café, his face drained of color, was the only one who turned to look toward the esplanade. The one who seemed to be in charge was tall, with a small head, a straight nose, and a scar across his cheek. He had a thick mustache and was wearing a shiny jacket and a wide-brimmed hat with a feather. A still-smoking rifle was slung across his shoulder. He had someone open a bottle and downed half of it in one swallow. He wiped his mouth with the back of his hand. From now on I'll be able to enjoy what I never had before: a bed ten spans wide so I can sleep lengthwise or crosswise. Whichever way I want. And in the next room I'll keep myself some captives, two or three rich man's whores who will pay homage to yours truly with fearful faces and gowns that leave their tiny breasts exposed. He turned to face us: The guy we just dispatched along with his adopted son was my cousin, the owner of all the vineyards in this county. We only intended to kill the old man, but the son wanted to hug his father one last time, so we sent them both to heaven in an eternal embrace.

The man in charge sat down at our table, and after staring at it with a vacant look for a few moments, he gave the cat a kick, sending it tumbling toward the door. I am the heir. And he shouted: A bottle! And glasses! One of the men pointed to the floor. There are no glasses. The man in charge looked at the old man. Instead of parading about with that stuffed animal that's already given you everything it had, you'd be better off if you came with us and cleaned our rifles, that goes for you too, kid! The barrel of my rifle is always hot and I wouldn't want it cooling off before this war is won. The cat man laughed so hard he seemed about to break, and everyone stopped drinking to stare at him, and then the cat man said that none of them were their father's sons. A scrawny man wearing a blue shirt and a red scarf around his neck lunged toward him, brandishing a bottle, threatening to smash it over his head if he repeated such nonsense. It's not me, it's that boy who said so; according to him, parents merely create a child's flesh and bones and with its first cry, the infant is infused with a soul that has been waiting for that moment. The tallest man in the group gave me a cold stare: Show us the soul! I stood up, charged into the scrawny man, who was blocking my way, and bolted out of there, tripping on the cat and sending it flying onto the countertop. The cat man meowed and meowed. Outside the fog had thickened, and perhaps that is why they didn't kill me, though they shot at me like maniacs.

XXIX

THE HERMIT

I SAW HIM AT ONCE, THE MAN TILLING THE FIELD. AND HE SAW me, for, shading his eyes with his hand and shouting loudly, he asked if I was headed to the chapel. Without giving me a chance to respond, he explained that the chapel was farther up, above the holm-oak forest, behind a thicket of strawberry trees and heather. Treading on clods of turned earth, he moved closer, and when he was standing next to me, he pushed his cap back. He's not like the rest of us. Who? I asked. Aren't you on your way to see the hermit? No. Well, you should pay him a visit. He's the grandest man on this earth. A giant. Not even the most angelic of angels can compare to him. His eyes were already filled with God when he arrived in these parts, he already breathed the breath of God . . . The chapel was in ruins, the ceiling had caved in, and two of the walls were gone. It was a den of serpents and lizards. The previous hermit had died of old age years ago. And this man, of whom I can only say that he is a saint, arrived here in a wretched state, skin and bones, barely able to stand, but with his sight set on the heavens. I went about helping him at once: Though I never had much of anything to spare, I took him whatever I could . . . a sliver of lard, a crust of bread, even if it meant I would have little to feed the chickens that night. Sometimes a few apples, sometimes a pot of honey. One day, without daring to look at me, the hermit told me he had prayed that God would reward me for the good I was doing him, and apparently God had conveyed to him the message that I would be admitted into His saintly glory on the day I breathed my last. And I live in peace. Ever since then, my vegetable garden has been the lushest, without even watering it, really, because as soon as it is thirsty the sky sends down rain. I harvest more grapes than ever. The earth is soft and black. And, as I work, my spirit lifts heavenward toward the blue and the clouds.

A few days after the saintly man's arrival, he began to gather stones: A wall was going up. He placed one of the stones—the longest and narrowest, which had been half buried near the Pinetell springs—crosswise above the portal, to serve as a lintel. And he covered it all with brick tiles which he had limped over to the abandoned farmhouse to collect. When he had completed work on the chapel, he built an altar from the trunk of an oak tree that had been felled by lightning; he dragged it to the site with a chain I lent him. And on that altar, where he says Mass every day at dawn, he placed a cross like the cross our Savior died on, made from four different kinds of wood: palm, cypress, olive, and cedar. On one side of the cross he keeps a crown of brambles and on the other, three rusted nails held together with a wire, their heads flattened. The Mass he says is unlike most: It seems that an angel—always the same one—serves as his altar boy and blows to enlarge the chapel, sheathing it with a glass veil until it becomes a cathedral. The day he dies, birds will usher him to the heavens—up, up—some pulling, others pushing . . . and they will lay him on a shipcloud wreathed in a pearly light. It'll do you good to see him. They say we are at war, that brothers are killing brothers, but here the God of grass and trees, sky and fog, water and rock continues to bless tender-hearted men. Go to the chapel. Go.

The path winded up among trees with tormented trunks and stiff, shimmering leaves. Through the trees I caught a glimpse of the chapel, entirely of stone, with moss-covered tiles. By the entrance sat a man wearing a garment of sackcloth, with a string around his neck at the end of which hung a cross made of dark wood. A rope, the whole of it a rosary of knots, encircled his waist. He raised his head and greeted me. I heard footsteps . . . he stretched out his arm. At his feet lay a basket full of beans. I told him my story. As though he hadn't heard a word, he issued an order: Help me sort these. The sky above our heads was fretted with small clouds. Along the path I had taken now came a young girl with a large basket. She set it on the ground next to us and took out a loaf of bread and a pot of jam. Without uttering one sad word, she turned and started back down. We cooked the beans on a shivering campfire in the middle of a clearing, in a pot that looked like gold. After lunch I doused the fire with a couple of buckets of water. Then he had me sit beside him and, examining me with his sickly eyes, he began to speak.

My father was a wealthy man. It was my constant misbehavior that put him in his grave. I was always asking him for money, and when he refused to give me any, I forged his signature. I appropriated his name for my own use. I inherited his fortune, but quickly squandered it. Mired in debt, having never worked a day in my life, I saw my friends soon vanish. Scorned by everyone who had surrounded me when my cup overflowed with wealth and plenty, I crumbled. I lodged in a miserable pension until I could no longer afford even that. I could have sought employment only as a stevedore, a porter, a street sweeper, a sign walker . . . a house painter? I wouldn't have known where to start. I stayed indoors during the day to avoid being seen. I wandered the streets at night. In the end, penniless, I took to sleeping fitfully on benches in train stations or in the street, until the first grey streamers of dawn appeared. On one of those nights, a manhole cover slid open, revealing a wreck of a man. With his help I got a job cleaning sewer lines. No one saw me, no one laughed at me. A hatred toward lordly people began to grow inside of me, a hatred toward all those who had money as I once had and whom I now considered my enemy. I loathed sumptuous houses, bejeweled women who were like window displays of rubies and diamonds. The people who had seen me on my knees, at their feet, and with a gesture of a richly ornamented finger and a look that wiped me from the face of the earth, had left me alone with myself.

Like roots whose reach is unknown, the sewer lines coiled beneath the houses of the rich and powerful. My comrades in misery were a resigned lot . . . I soon parted ways with them, not because of what they were like, but because I needed to be alone. When I heard someone approaching, I escaped deeper into the sewer. I moved about with a lantern around my neck and carried an iron rod that I banged on the cement vault in my longing to destroy the very foundations of the city. I could feel the remotest sewer lines beckoning me. I spent hour upon hour begrimed, breathing in the foulness of that dark labyrinth that collected the filth of the city. On stormy days the water carried dead rats out to sea. Sometimes my exalted hatred would abate and tears would stream down my cheeks. And then I yearned to breathe the air that I had denied myself. I would search for an exit without finding one. I had no way of knowing beneath which streets, which places I prowled, drenched in putrid water, surrounded by rats that spied on me from hidden crevices. I don't know how long I lived that way . . . until one day I felt the iron rungs of a ladder piercing the soles of my feet. The manhole cover was heavy; my arms were like reeds, my hands like claws. My neck could barely hold my head up. It was a spring night; the air rustled the leaves. I was near the sea and the smell of tar . . .

When I came to I was lying on a bunk, all of my senses focused on the sound of lapping water, without the strength to ask myself how I had arrived there. Every now and then I heard the woeful wailing of a siren. I glimpsed a group of officers in a brightly lit room, dressed in white, drinking and laughing. I climbed down a rope ladder and untied the boat.

In the middle of the sea, the sky lulled me, the moon blanched me. Caressed by the sky and the night, alone with my misery, my anger slowly turning into a meaningless word, I discovered what I did not know I had been seeking: to reach God by following the arduous path of life. A beach welcomed me. Kneeling on the sand, I accepted life. I needed to be reborn, to expunge the dictates that men—both the powerful and the powerless—had forced on me. And suddenly, like an immaculate lamb, our Savior, the one who gives all things, revealed Himself to me in the center of the sun.

I traversed village after village, treading upon paths of tender grass, across sowed fields, along riverbanks. I punished myself: I did not eat when hungry, nor drink when thirsty. I drew blood by flogging myself with stinging nettles . . . at death's door, without quite dying, I blessed the tender shoot, the fallen feather, the heart of the flower, the slug and the leech, the green snake and the earth-colored snake, the cascading water, the acorn that satiates the wild boar's hunger . . . and here in this light-infused solitude, gazing at a sun that burns my eyes, in the company of the Cross, upon this friendly earth from which came the clay I was made of, surrounded by life that is robust and secret, I exist in a state of love, so that God might not forsake me.

XXX

ANOTHER FARMHOUSE

I CLIMBED AN OLD TREE WHOSE TRUNK, FORTUNATELY, HAD KNOTS that I could use as footholds, for when I found myself near the farmhouse three dogs appeared, barking loudly and charging at me. Below my perch, a table was set for about a hundred people. After a while, the dogs tired of barking and trying to climb the tree and rushed off to greet some girls with baskets who were walking in my direction. They started arranging bread rolls, glasses, wineglasses, and plates around the table. Two little girls who had been hiding behind a well began to scream and plodded over to the tree where I was ensconced. Between two fingers the oldest was holding an earthworm that coiled and uncoiled. She placed it on the ground, and the two of them started poking it with twigs. The slick, red worm kept squirming. They didn't leave it alone until it had been pulled to pieces. The girls with the baskets were busy coming and going. The little girls again hid behind the well screaming, Another worm! Another worm! Let's kill it! Let's kill it! Above my head, a bird watched me, wings spread and head forward.

There was music. Young men and girls arrived in wagons, trucks, and carts. I moved farther up the tree and straddled a branch that, although thick, creaked as though it were about to break. The young people climbed down from the vehicles and started dancing and jumping around the threshing floor. Shortly thereafter, trucks filled with militiamen appeared, one of them loaded with rifles and machine guns. The last to arrive was a truck festooned with white flowers, and from it descended the bride and groom, both in militia attire. She wore a white flower in her hair. Long live the bride and groom! Viva the bride and groom! The guests surrounded them shouting long live the bride and groom. The bride, short and stout, laughed continuously, and the groom, tall and thin, pushing aside those who got too close, kept saying: enough, enough . . . Everyone began to take their places at the table. More cries were heard—the parents! The parents! An elderly couple descended from a cart pulled by a palomino. The mother wore a mantilla, the father a black hat. The parents are here! The parents are here! The groom's parents! The girls who had set the table brought out *porrons* of wine. Viva the groom's parents! Soon, women bearing food emerged from the farmhouse and placed on the table platters stacked high with slices of cured sausage, different varieties of ham, mounds of shelled prawns, open muscles with pink sauce, clams drowned in green sauce, and lobster tails garnished with mayonnaise. Two brawny men appeared with bowls of salad—lettuce and tomato with green and black olives—and plates piled with roasted eggplant and red peppers. Everyone talked and laughed, everyone was happy, everyone was hungry, everyone raised *porrons* and glasses, shouting over and over, long live the bride and groom, so there would be no end to the couple's happiness or the Perarnau family name. A few young men rose from their chairs, approached the bride, and kissed her on both cheeks. A place at the head of the table remained empty, but everyone ignored it until the bride pointed to it and the two brawny men glanced at each other, sprang up and made for the house. The dinner guests turned their heads to see what was happening. The two men soon reappeared with a lardy man, round as a full moon, holding him by the arms to help him walk. The man, ruddy-faced, with close-set eyebrows, was wearing corduroy trousers that were so wide they resembled a skirt. And espadrilles with black ribbon ties. Arms aloft, he cried: I haven't eaten for more than two hours, I'm hungry and weak. He walked without being able to see his feet or where he placed them, so large was his paunch. When he reached the well, he stopped to catch his breath and the girls cropped up like two little devils and hurled a worm at his head. Scoundrels! Scoundrels! And he started weeping, saying he was scared to walk because his brothers were unthinking brutes who would let him trip on a stone, and that would be the end of him. There are no stones, there are no stones, said one of the brothers; the other lost his patience and shouted, walk, you fool, walk! I swear there are no stones in your way. Come here, Uncle, come here, shouted the bride, holding up a fork with a prawn speared on it. We want Manel over here! A man as burly as the two escorting the moon-shaped man stepped toward the brothers. Mind the stones! Whenever they take him out for some fresh air, he's afraid of tripping—said a girl holding a glass of blood-red wine to her mouth—and falling flat on his round belly, and rolling and rolling, with those short little arms and legs of his. The moon-shaped man lowered his head. They plopped him down in his assigned spot, on two chairs that had been pushed together, the backrests and crosspieces held together with wires. A bowl of hors d'oeuvres and another with salad and roasted red peppers was set before him. Women and girls kept removing the empty dishes and returning with food-laden platters. And then it was time for the chicken and the grilled meat, the partridge and the quail. The moon-shaped man, who had eyes only for the food he was ingesting, ate the hors d'oeuvres and salad, followed by two plates of rice with hunks of pork and rabbit legs, two monkfish, two hakes, two chickens stuffed with pears and prunes, half a veal round, three partridges, and two squabs . . . a platter of sweets, a ring cake, three dishes of *crema catalana* and who knows how many flans. After coffee was served, the dance began on the threshing floor. While everyone was dancing, the bride and groom climbed in the truck with the rifles and machine guns and drove away, raising a cloud of dust. When the guests who were dancing realized, they began to reprimand the couple: That's not fair! You cheats! A girl with a red skirt and a red flower in her hair shouted until she was hoarse, Viva the bride and groom! Viva! as she twirled a bunch of colorful ribbons against the paling sun.

One of my legs ached and I changed positions. The branch groaned. The moon-shaped man glanced up, searching among the leaves. When he spotted me, he seemed fascinated by what he saw, and he raised his arm and motioned for me to come down. He had me sit beside him and asked me to get him a glass of water and sugar; he couldn't reach the pitcher, much less the sugar bowl. Lunch has made me thirsty. As he gulped down the water, he kept looking at me with pitiful eyes. He told me to eat, he said I looked hungry. I stuffed myself with sweets, with cake, with a bit of crème brûlée that someone hadn't finished.

Here you have me, a man consumed by a never-ending urge to eat. The men who were holding me by the arms are my brothers: the middle one and the youngest. They are waiting for me to die, claws at the ready. I used to eat like a bird, I had no appetite, my growth was stunted. My mother was always preparing delicacies for me . . . here, have some chicken livers, have some lamb brains, have some hen combs, have some rabbit cheeks. All light fare, which I scarcely ever touched. I was scrawny. All skin and bones, arms like matchsticks, legs like matchsticks. Until someone told my mother to feed me honey. I had never tasted it before, and I liked it so much that all day long I would cry for more. I kept pots of it beside my bed and spent my nights dipping fingers into it, licking away. And, being small of frame, I slowly developed a considerable layer of fat. This change went hand in hand with my brothers' glee as I turned into a ball of lard and they saw how any little effort left me winded. In the end they deemed me worthless, even though I had married and produced a son (everybody shouted Miracle! because no one could understand how I had managed to make the boy). My wife and son soon died, and my brothers cast me aside and managed the property without offering me any explanations, although I was the heir. I have seven months to live; my heart has a casing of fat that is slowly choking it. Suddenly, he ordered me to climb back up the tree because his brothers were coming for him and they would scold him if they saw him talking to a stranger.

The two men took him back to the house the same way they had helped him to the table: holding him by the arms and prodding him occasionally from behind. The dancers had left and everything lay enveloped in the shadows of dusk. As I climbed down from the tree I scared off a clutch of sparrows that were pecking at the bread crumbs around the table. The dogs were eating by the portal; this time they didn't chase after me, perhaps because after seeing me talking to the moon-shaped man they counted me as one of their own.

I raised my head, baa . . . baa . . . baa . . . those sheep cries intrigued me; I had to see for myself what was happening. Behind the farmhouse, near the vegetable garden, three stout men were shearing sheep. The animals had wide foreheads, pointy muzzles, droopy ears, and legs so covered in wool that you could scarcely see them. The men had rough faces. One of them, with white hair and a deeply furrowed brow, immediately spotted me. When I realized he had seen me I made an attempt to flee, which spoiled everything because then the younger one, in a fleece vest, grabbed me by the arm and shoved me to the ground. I kicked him. But he was the stronger of the two. He dragged me to where the sheep were being sheared and, amid shouts and panting, they pinned me down by the arms and legs and started running the shears over my head.

I awoke at daybreak. I was lying by a hayloft. A hen was pecking at my feet. A rooster crowed. I ran a hand over my head, bald in patches, unshorn in others. I would have stayed there and slept forever, buried in the hay. But I had to leave. I was sore, everything ached. I stood up and started walking, though not without first turning around to bid farewell to the farmhouse where the wedding party had taken place. From a ground floor window the moon-shaped man, his face as red as a partridge, craned his neck forward as he looked at me and blew his nose between two fingers.

XXXI

Matilda's White Belly

I TRIED LOOKING AT THE SUN, THE WAY THE HERMIT DID, TO SEE if it would burn my pupils. This game of mine was interrupted by the racket of a motorcycle that came to a sudden halt in front of me. The man on the motorcycle said, if you want me to take you somewhere don't hesitate to ask, I'm not going anywhere. His mouth warped into a grimace of disgust. He had long teeth, his canines much like a dog's, and restless eyes that darted around without focusing on anything. Can't make up your mind? He removed a pack of cigarettes from his jacket pocket and held it out to me as he said, someone really worked you over, son. He stuck the cigarettes under my nose, determined that I take one; I had to confess I had never smoked before, other than some herbs behind my mother's back when I was little and trying to act like a man. Smoke! The first drag made me cough. My eyes watered. The motorcycle man said he liked to smoke fast so he could get to the end of the cigarette and light another one. The best part is when you light up. That's why men who have lost their eyesight don't smoke . . . when I tire of smoking I'll fix this mess of a haircut you've got. Who the hell did that to you? I liked him because his eyes darted from the branches to me, from the road to the grass, from the tip of his cigarette to the tip of mine, which was turning to ash.

He began his story by saying that he had once had a brig inside a bottle and that it was his father's fault that he had chosen to become a barber: When he was small, his father would have him cut the hair on the back of his neck because he couldn't reach there. Then I was hired as an apprentice to the barber two doors down, a sad, bald man who had a liver condition and subsisted on a diet of boiled rice. He died when I finished my military service and I took over the barbershop. All the clients knew me, and they continued to come. I had two shop windows, one facing the main street and the other an alleyway. They were lined with empty bottles labelled quinine and tar, and a giant bottle that had once held cologne and that I filled with water. On the corner in front of the barbershop was a bakery. When my boss died, the baker followed suit. Two months later, a flower shop opened where the bakery had been. It took me a while to notice the owner. Then, one Saint Magdalene's Day, tired of hearing my Magdalena whine that I never brought her any gifts, I went in to buy her a rose. She was a manicurist, Magdalena. She came to the house on Sundays; we'd sleep together for a while and then we'd clean the place. Magdalena was a quiet girl from a modest but decent family.

The owner of the flower shop wrapped the rose in tinfoil and spritzed it with water. Her eyes changed colors and her skin was silkier than the plush petals of the rose she had just sold me. From that day on I started spying on her from behind the giant bottle. She had the appearance of a little girl with sword-like legs. She always wore a black skirt and a white blouse. Until finally I could contain myself no longer and I strode into the shop to buy a begonia that I would put—I told her—in the main shop window. You'll need to water it often. With the begonia as an excuse, I would stop in to see her every now and then. The leaves are falling off. I don't think I'm watering it enough. Her name was Matilda. I fell in love with her. I left Magdalena.

I didn't want Matilda to work. I wanted her all to myself. Sell the flower shop. But no, there she was, as always, with her boxes of flowers and the atomizer she used to spritz them. I won't recount the wedding night, I'll only say she was still wearing her black skirt and white blouse when she got in bed. I unzipped her. She had nothing on underneath. I'd never seen a belly as white as hers. It took my breath away. And every night I worshiped it. I never tired of looking at it. I abandoned my friends, I stopped playing billiards. There weren't enough nights, not enough Sunday afternoons or holidays to worship and worship and worship her belly. I lost clients. I never stopped asking her to give up her shop. It was a silent war. Sell the store, sell the store. But she wouldn't budge. Until, disappointed and defeated, I learned to keep quiet. One evening, about three months after I had stopped talking to her, she remained standing on the other side of the table after serving me dinner, eyes downcast, and then she suddenly lifted her skirt and stood there with her belly exposed. I continued to eat as if nothing had happened, as if she were in the kitchen preparing something. And from that evening on, every night at dinnertime she would do the same: skirt up and belly showing. I stopped having supper at home. I stopped having lunch at home. I went to the bar, I played billiards, I returned home at dawn. She never relented. She would show me her belly when I climbed into bed, when I came out from washing, as soon as I opened my eyes. I grew sick of her. And then, fortunately, the war started. I enlisted at once. And now I serve as liaison, or at least I did. I deserted, left my battalion. I think I might open a barbershop in France. Want to come with me? I told him I preferred to be on my own so I could consider things slowly, methodically. Clicking his tongue, he strode to his motorcycle and from the haversack hanging on the back brought out a clipper and a razor. He left my head looking like a ball and my face fuzz-free. He departed enveloped by a cloud of dust. When the dust settled I saw a strange man coming toward me.

XXXII

The Man Who Walked with His Back to the Sun and the Moon

HE WAS IN HIS MIDDLE YEARS. HIS BLACK BEARD CAME DOWN TO his chest and his grey hair reached the middle of his back. He was bare-chested beneath a jacket with moth-eaten lapels. The legs of his trousers had rips of considerable size, one around the knee, the other at thigh-level. He wore new sandals. A rusty key hung from a string around his neck. His eyes sparkled as though made of silver, and his lips were barely visible beneath the tangled hairs of his mustache. A blackbird was perched on his shoulder. He stopped in front of me, stood there for a while, and then asked me if I knew the name of the nearest village. It occurred to me that he was in a jesting mood, but what he really wanted, like most people, was someone to talk to. Someone to lend him an ear. The blackbird squawked. Stop being a nuisance. The sun, he said, is retiring and there will be no shadows. When the moon is out I shall be on my way. My grandmother was very old when she died, but dead and dressed in her Sunday best she had all the freshness of flowers; it was as though she had fallen asleep after coming home from Mass. She taught me to love my shadow. She said: You and your shadow were placed in the saddle of life so that you might gallop together. I have no one in this world, nor do I wish to; I want to live alone with my shadow. I was little then. Haven't you noticed that you have a shadow? I didn't move and the shadow didn't move. It was I who cast that dark smudge on the ground. I make the shadow. I am it. No. It is you. Without it—and she pressed a finger against my forehead—you would not be. If you lose it, you die. Whenever I found myself alone I stood in front of the lamp and slowly lifted an arm, and so did the shadow. I extended the other arm, so did the shadow. I was little. I tilted my head, it did the same. Everything I did, it did as well.

Shadows suck the spirits, the soul-sap, from grass and roots. I want to see the spirits. That cannot be. The shadows also feed on defunct ants and on carcasses of oxen, which infect them with their fury. Examine yours in the moonlight, when frogs are quiet and water snakes slither across the mud . . . your shadow will gild the lilies and paint the roses. When you are grown, and in the company of your shadow, you will hear the cries of unborn creatures, the breathing of the world, the screaming of the stars. My grandmother had young hands, and even on the eve of her death her eyes gleamed with mischief. She died, but could not be buried when she should have been: The casket maker was ill, and no one else in the village, or in any of the neighboring villages, could pick up a plane or a handsaw because no one knew how to take wood and turn it into a pine box. One afternoon, at that time of day when the heat is at its most oppressive, I raised the blinds after watching her for a while as she lay dead. A ray of sunlight fell on her. I stood in front of the window and let my shadow keep her company until the sun set.

~~

I studied, I lived, I never again remembered I had once had a grandmother. I became a public defender, working for the poor, the castaways, those who had been incarcerated for stealing a piece of bread. Always in endless conversations, endless consolations, my nose always clogged by tormented breaths, my ears filled with all the misery and misfortune of the world. The blackbird squawked three times and the man whacked it on the wing. Hush! I lived in a ground-floor lodging with three rooms, all three a pigsty, with dust and spiderwebs everywhere, rubbish never taken out on time, dishes piled on the stovetop and floor, glistening beetles, and dirty clothes strewn over chairs. One night on my way home I realized that I was walking down my street all alone. The doors were bolted, windows too. I passed a street lamp . . . my shadow had vanished. I stopped short and instinctively raised an arm: The arm had no shadow. I arrived home riddled with anguish, just as the moon was coming out. I turned my back to it, and the faint glimmer of that winter moon—to see it was to believe it—deposited my own shadow at my feet. As I inserted the key I am now wearing around my neck into the lock, the shadow rested on the doorframe and I stroked it many times. I wanted it to know I loved it. I left everything: wretched prisoners, widows' tears, orphans' despair, killers' remorse . . . and from that day on I have lived for my shadow alone. I don't want to ever lose it again, I want it to be mine, all mine. And that is why it should come as no surprise that, now that the moon is rising, I will take my leave of you and depart accompanied by my shadow. My back to the moon so I can see it at night, my back to the sun so I can see it by day. Farewell—*Adéu*.

XXXIII

THE BRICKLAYER

In front of a bombed-out house, its blackened walls still standing, a man paced back and forth, cursing and hitting himself on the head with his fists. More than seeing me, he must have sensed my presence, for he suddenly fell silent. He was bald on top but had lots of hair on the sides, and his bushy brows met in the middle of his forehead. He sat down on a chopping block, rested his hands on his thighs and raised his head: My wife was buried this morning. Mercifully, my son went to his grandparents' a week ago—yes, that must be why he was spared—and he doesn't know anything about the bombing or his mother's death. I was in the vineyard when the bomb fell. But, why? Why did they have to drop a bomb—just the one—here in this godforsaken town where there aren't even any young people left? His voice cracked: not even that . . . they just want to wreck people's lives. A woman like her, to die beneath the rubble of her own house, alone inside the house, never having harmed a soul . . . The day I die, if I go with a lucid mind, I will be thinking of her still, my Eulàlia. And—you see?—my heart aches, but I don't feel she's really dead. It can't be so, I can sense her moving about, conscientious as always, scrubbing, sewing, mending, striving to keep the house as clean as a whistle, everything in shipshape order . . . If it weren't for the fact that my son is still a boy, and as good as his mother, I'd rather just die. Since I married her I have known only joy, never a moment of vexation. And that's saying a lot. Look at these hands. Clearly the hands of a bricklayer, are they not? The skin cracked and rough from handling bricks, burnt by the cement. We built this house with our own sweat, by saving every cent we had to purchase now a sack of cement, now a couple of sacks of sand, now a batch of bricks. We spared no expense! Poor Estanislau, the plasterer, came and wouldn't charge me for the material or the work. And Jeremies, the electrician, came and refused his wages. And Manel, the carpenter, came and donated the door and window frames. And Belloc, the painter, turned up and contributed the varnish. And then all of us, electrician, carpenter, plasterer, painter, and myself, went to work painting the whole thing—with blue shutters. Eulàlia made lunch for all of us. It was marvelous. You can't imagine the glory of building a house from the foundations to the roof. Of seeing it go up. Of picking up a brick, slapping cement on three sides and—plop!—there you have it, ready to set. And one by one, putting up the rafters and covering them, building walls as though it were easy as pie . . . Laying shingles, some belly up, others down—there—gutters and paths for the rain to sing through. He eyed me for a while and then averted his gaze. Behind me stood a thin boy, tan from being out-of-doors fighting in the war, for it was plain that that was what he had been doing: His arm was bandaged, forehead too. I, he said, weep for this man's house and for the death of his wife. Though I'm much younger, we have always been like brothers. My name is Jeremies and I'm an electrician. I had scarcely learned the trade when I was handed a rifle, and from then on it was life in the open for me, hounded by Moors—who are as treacherous as they come—and one day, finding myself cornered without even knowing how to shoot, I pulled the trigger and a bullet came out and the Moor stumbled before falling to the ground. The fright of having killed a man sent me running, and then it was I who stumbled from two bullets that were chasing me, one of which grazed my arm, the other my forehead, and from there it was straight to the hospital, which had been bombed three times despite the white sheet with a red cross on the rooftop . . . If this fellow misses putting up walls, he said, I miss doing the wiring, running the wires through the grooves, sliding them along and along so that the lightbulbs will light up. A man younger than the bricklayer and older than the electrician approached us and began speaking in a low voice, as though he were at confession. I volunteered and now I've lost everything: shop and tools. Tools I had bought, one by one, as an apprentice, and tools my father had given me little by little, starting with the chisel. Just ask—I had them all: hammer, saw, and handsaw. And the plane, which made shavings so delicate they resembled the ringlets on one of those giant female figures we parade around in processions . . . always planing doors that don't fit or shutters that are too large, so that everything will open and close properly, everything will work as it should . . . When I mentioned that I had a carnation field they said that that was all well and good but it was more important to have a vegetable garden, especially in wartime, when you never know if there will be anything to eat the following day. This war is a terrible calamity, can anyone tell me why we are fighting? The bricklayer said it was to beat back the enemy, but then the carpenter pointed out that, to our enemies, we are the enemy. The electrician said: Even if we win this war it'll be as though we've lost it, the way a war is set up, everyone loses. The hearth builder joined us and said that we could cry all we wanted and there would still be nothing to plow, we were all cannon fodder, nothing but cannon fodder. The bricklayer raised his head. Three men were coming our way pushing wheelbarrows loaded with picks and shovels and bricklayer's hammers. They were the painter, the plasterer, and the carpenter's son, coming to help rebuild the house. They immediately stepped inside the ruins; I did the same. Until it was dark and the bricklayer said, should we stop for supper? We all went to the church. The bricklayer lit a lantern and set it on the altar. There were no saints. The pews were piled up in a corner; the plasterer picked one up and, with the carpenter's help, smashed it and used it to build a fire on the floor. When it's all over I'll make nicer pews than these. They put a pot of white beans garnished with strips of bacon on the fire.

The carpenter asked the bricklayer if he knew me. No. He was just passing by and we got to talking. Soon the bricklayer and I found ourselves alone. Time for bed now. We stretched out on the floor. I hadn't been asleep for two hours when a voice woke me. Go home.

At daybreak everyone was back at work. I spent three days helping them pile up the rubble and remove the cement from the bricks, but on what would have been the fourth day I left them, not so much to get away from them, but to get away from the voice that woke me every night as soon as I fell asleep, go home, go home . . .

XXXIV

A Victim

A GIRL WAS CRYING BY A FOUNTAIN. ON HEARING MY FOOTSTEPS she raised her tearful eyes and covered her face with her hands as though wanting to hide her whole being from me. The water sang as it flowed and slipped away among the ferns. I didn't know what to do, whether to walk on or stop and console the girl. She had her sleeves rolled up, exposing a bruise on both arms, above her elbows. I sat down near her. She backed away, stared at me and— like a shard of glass that suddenly shines in the sunlight—a bolt flashed across her eyes, I couldn't be sure whether of fear or rage. She stood, sat back down, rose again, drank from the fountain while holding her hair back with one hand, sat down again, stood back up, and just as I was starting to think that she was about to go, she knelt before me and began to weep so helplessly that leaving her then would have required a heart of stone. Between sobs, she told me her name. Lena. Bent over, with her arms on my thighs and her head down, she confided in a low voice that her troubles all stemmed from her marriage. Look! She stood and showed me her bruises. Look! You see? My husband. I didn't want to get married, I just wanted us to be sweethearts. He insisted we get married. I was only fifteen, I didn't want to marry. He made me. Then came what I feared most: A husband is not a fiancé. He wasn't the same person, he had become someone else. Always talking about dinner not being ready, or being too hot, too cold . . . or not wanting it reheated . . . How can he expect not to find it re-heated, she said, raising her head with a desperate look, if I never know when he's coming home at night? The fish, he sometimes finds overdone, others undercooked. Vegetables, always overcooked. The meat is never tender enough, you let them cheat you at the shops; the peaches they gave you are bruised, you let them take advantage of you; this oil isn't olive oil, you let yourself be swindled. You didn't pull the sheets tight, the wrinkles kept me from sleeping. There aren't any clean shirts . . . why aren't you doing the laundry? This shirt is poorly ironed, what's on your mind when you're handling that iron? And he drinks. He's turned into a human cask filled with trodden grapes. And he wears me out. It's true that sometimes I haven't done the washing because I've been ill, and sometimes I've had to make the bed in a hurry because I'm behind on my chores. And why is that? Go up to the village, go down to the other village to fetch some potatoes, or beans, or a bit of rice. Go over to that town, go over to that other town to pick up a few chunks of soap . . . because the war . . . scoldings are my daily bread, they're making me ill, making me wish to die, and I can only find consolation by talking about my woes at the fountain . . . and she wept and wept with her head on my knees.

Through the trees I glimpsed a shadow drawing nearer. It was Lena's husband—whose name, Magí, I already knew—looking exhausted and disarmingly innocent. He took me by the arm and led me under a willow tree. She's been grumbling about me, hasn't she? That's all she does. I am an upright man, and a teetotaler, whatever she may say. She tells lies. She strings them together, one after the other. I married her because at age fifteen she found herself alone in the world, and I wanted to protect her. What would have become of her if I hadn't taken her in? And I was desperately in love, too. But I'd been deceived. She wasn't sweet, she wasn't good. It was as though she had led a two-faced existence all her life, since childhood, and her duplicity was revealed once we were married. She's a relentless faultfinder and name-caller, always accusing me of being up to no good, saying that if I come home late it's because I'm mixed up in some trouble. I'm a mechanic and didn't go to war because I'm missing a lung. She's lazy, always about to pounce on me, claws ready, like a frenzied cat. One day a while back, at my wits' end, I finally slapped her across the face, leaving her cheek flushed. Has she shown you the bruises on her arms? I caused them, yes, by pushing her away after she sprung herself on me trying to gouge out my eyes. She doesn't put food on the table—she hurls it. The vegetables spill out of the serving dish; the stew flies out of the tureen. But in front of others she plays the poor unfortunate lamb . . . and because she has the face of an angel just descended from the heavens, she has everyone's sympathy. She has gone so far as to make people believe she was forced to marry a crook against her will. I spend nights wandering the streets, afraid to enter my own home. I never know what awaits me there, what she will hurl at me next. I walk the streets aimlessly until the small hours of the morning, by the haylofts, along the vegetable gardens . . . dogs follow me, birds take flight when they hear me coming. And I'm always on the verge of pulling out my hair because of the awful mistake I made in marrying poor, poor Lena. Take a look at her—a good, long look . . . We stepped closer. Lena was bent over crying, her tears mixing with the clear water that rushed to hide beneath the earth, and she peered at us out of the corner of her eye, with a touch of mischief on her lips that seemed to hold the threat of making her husband's existence a living hell. I left them.

I turned around after a while and saw them walking slowly in the fading light of dusk, their arms around each other.

⤛

That night, and for many more nights thereafter, I dreamed of Eva. She was standing in front of the reeds calling my name.

PART
THREE

XXXV

THE RED EARTH

THE PATH WAS SHORT AND NARROW. IT STARTED AT A BEND IN THE
road and was furrowed by ditches and strewn with upturned stones.
On the left side, ensconced among cypress and cedar trees, was the
garden of an old home. The fence around it—sharp-tipped wooden
posts held together by rusty wire—was nearly concealed by a great
thicket of honeysuckle, behind which grew a row of lilacs laden
with clusters of dry seed. On the right side of the path, beyond a
waterless fountain, was the courtyard of a massive farmhouse, lined
with thirsty, withering, red and pink geraniums. Under an arbor,
near a henless coop, lay a dead cat. The sun fell full on the façade,
which was adorned with a sundial of yellow and blue tiles with a
motif of branches and leaves. It was exactly noon. The path led to a
square with only three houses, adjoined, shingles blackened, doors
wide open as if everyone were out in the fields. In front of the houses, by a patch of red earth that was also crisscrossed by ditches, a
waterless horse trough served me as a seat. Nearby, a cart full of
hay lay on its side in a pool of blood. Standing in front of one of the
houses, I cupped my mouth with my hands and shouted. No one
answered. I shouted in front of one of the other houses as well: The
echo returned my voice. I let out a third cry. Again, no one replied,
so I entered, practically on tiptoe. On a round, skirted table was
a carafe full of still-tepid coffee and a basket with a few slices of
black bread. Just as I had done at the house with the mirror in

the foyer, I salted the bread before dousing it with olive oil. Not a sound could be heard, only my chewing and the soughing of the wind, just enough of a breeze to sweep in a few dead leaves, a few motes of dust.

I didn't see him at first because the bed was blocking my view. In a bedroom on the second floor lay a dead man, his open eyes staring at the ceiling. On one of his hands—short fingers, black nails—a fly was grooming its legs. The man had a wound in the middle of his chest, and the entire front of his shirt was crimson. In the next house, the furniture had been turned upside down, the clothes in the closets flung on the floor and trampled on, as if someone had danced on top of them. I entered the last house: In the fireplace in the bedroom I found some half-burnt papers and, by the balcony, a shotgun with a metal-studded butt. A French door with smashed windowpanes gave onto a courtyard lined with empty flower pots. Lying on one of the flower pots was a bald, eyeless doll with a deflated ball by her hand.

In the distance, endless mountains, the full spectrum of greys and blues. The peace of the earth breathed all around me. From so much looking, I could no longer see. From so much listening, I could no longer hear. Everything—mountains, houses, path, water trough—merged together and with me. I did not want to think of blood: I became one with everything.

At the end of the square the path continued. Half of a snake lay in my way—the tail half. A wheel must have split it in two, flinging the head into the woods. The path was not straight and, toward the middle of it, in front of some pine trees heavy with caterpillar clusters, I heard water flowing. The path then widened, ending in a village square bordered by an iron railing. The valley that extended beyond was a tract of vivid patches of land that died at the foot of a wooded mountain. At the lookout point I leaned over the railing and recoiled in horror. Just beneath me was a large, recently-dug pit filled with bodies—legs, arms, heads, guts—and heaps of red earth piled up on the sides, mixed with picks and shovels . . . the whole a tangled mess streaked with blood and blood puddles that glistened in the singularly translucent light of that day. I fled, my head spinning. At the top of the path, by the honeysuckle, I vomited, disgorging all my bile.

The cleft snake again blocked my path. For two days and two nights I did not eat or drink, as I shoveled earth over the dead. Until they were covered. Before leaving them I faced the waning moon and entrusted their souls to God.

XXXVI

FEAR

SOMEONE HAD BEEN FOLLOWING ME FOR A WHILE, BUT I COULD
not remember when or where this someone had started to trail me.
I couldn't hear anything, not the sound of footsteps, not the rustling of leaves. And yet I was certain that someone was following
me and did not want me to notice him. I didn't dare turn around.
I scarcely dared to breathe. I carefully placed my feet where the
ground was barest to avoid the sound of crunching leaves. I could
feel my pulse pounding. Who could be following me? If the person
following me were real I would have heard him behind me and I
would have only had to turn around to see him. But I heard nothing. Clouds scurried by overhead. I stopped to listen better. Do
not turn around. The woods were at times flooded with light, at
times filled with thickening shadows. Had that someone stopped
when I stopped? It is asphyxiating to sense oneself being followed
through the heart of the forest, where something could be lurk-
ing behind every tree. Do *not* turn around, I warned myself. If
you turn around you will see something that is best unseen. If you
turn around, whoever is following you will realize that you have
noticed him. Do not let on that you have noticed him. Do not turn
around! Was that rustling in the branches a voice? I wanted to
run but I could not. My legs were frozen and I could not. A drop
of cold sweat rolled down my cheek. I had heard chilling tales of
horror, the kind that make your hairs stand on end. I had lived

through that night in the castle and those nights in the house with the mirror in the foyer. I am past the point of fear, I told myself. But the terror I experienced in that forest was of a different nature; it was as though the dead man my father had killed on the train tracks were about to jump out from behind a tree, determined to harm me.

The resemblance between fathers and sons had, upon occasion, caused me to reflect. If a father dies of a malady of the heart, the son dies of a malady of the heart; if a father dies with a sickened brain, the son dies with a sickened brain. I pinched my arm to make sure I was not delirious. That I was wide awake and crossing a densely wooded forest, and that it was not the first time I had done so. I had always found comfort in the solitude of the woods. I tapped my ears with the palms of my hands. I tried to swallow saliva but had none to swallow. I ran my tongue over lips drier than cardboard. Some time later, very slowly, I dared to turn my head and look back out of one eye. Behind me, the crepuscular gloaming had spawned castles of red and grey beneath a sun as round as a gold medal. Between that sun and myself, a mountain of wilderness. I would have liked to find myself surrounded by people on a street full of lights—a happy street, with women holding children's hands, with shop windows on either side—and to feel only the slightest of fears at the prospect of dying on that most unforeseeable of days. Why should I be afraid? I needed company. I made an effort to rid myself of fear, so that the evil that lurked behind me would not be the one to come and keep me company. I had become two people: the one sweating with fright and the one who believed there was no reason to be afraid. How could that be? I wanted to shout to drive away my fear but no sound issued from my mouth. The evening sky with its first stars was my enemy; it would come tumbling down on me to punish me for succumbing to fright on a night such as that. I sensed the ever stronger presence of that invisible someone powerful enough to read my thoughts. I suddenly let myself drop to the ground, my body curled into a ball, my eyes so wide they hurt. I must move, walk. Escape whatever it was that was weighing on me like a rock, slowly burying me beneath stones so large that I found myself powerless to dislodge them. I rose, holding on to a tree . . . to be a tree to be a cloud to be the wind. I thought I glimpsed a furtive beast in the distance, standing on its hind legs, ready to pounce on me. Beasts did not frighten me. I was unspeakably thirsty. I trudged along, dragging myself until I tripped and fell flat on my stomach. Nothing was real. I had never run away from home. Everything had been a dream. I was still in my bed dreaming, the intoxicating smell of carnations wafting through the open window. And yet, I could feel the beast spying on me and I was on the point of calling to it: come here, come. The shadows spread, effacing the contours of the branches. I could not remember how or when the day had begun; perhaps it had begun in the forest with that fear. Who had sucked the day's beginning from my consciousness? High above and far away a flock of birds cawed as they flew by. A moonbeam trembled at my feet. It seemed to me it was no longer I who was walking, but the trees, the entire forest. Had I entered the woods or had the woods entered me? I came to a clearing and found myself screaming as I crossed it, arms spread like the wings of the birds that had flown by. The fear was now of another kind: It was myself I feared. I was afraid of never being myself again, for the Great Fear was tightening its grip on me. The moonlight led me to the entrance of a cave. I entered with my arms extended in front of me, treading carefully until I reached the rock wall at the end. I pressed my back against it and let myself slip to the ground. I could glimpse a sliver of sky that was soon covered by a cloud. The blood began to flow through my veins again, my heart grew steadier. A small animal, perhaps a rabbit or a hare, bounded in as though it were being chased; it must have smelled me because it fled just as crazed as it had entered. A storm broke; the thunder and lightning came in quick, unrelenting succession, and the sky discharged water as though it were being emptied. I could not say if the rain lasted but a short moment or hours upon hours. The downpour made me feel safe and I fell into a deep slumber. And a dream entered my slumber: A giant hand approached through the rising waters and blocked the entrance to the cave so that I would never escape.

XXXVII

THE LAKE

THE DOWNPOUR HAD ENDED, BUT RAINDROPS CONTINUED TO FALL from trees and everything was shrouded in fog. Here and there, a tree trunk or shrub emerged from the milky whiteness, like a surprise. I was assailed by the smell of earth, the smell of decay from rains that had fallen on the leaves of countless autumns. The landscape changed; the gorse had been replaced by fern, and the terrain sloped. I heard the fluttering of bird wings. I sat down on a damp, moss-covered rock by a pond with rippling water. Perhaps one day—if I died near this spot where I had paused to sit—a hunter or a wanderer like myself would find, instead of the carcass of a wild animal, my own remains. With the tip of his boot he would unearth a bone, and beneath it would be an ant colony or a centipede's nest or perhaps a worm that would coil in desperation at being discovered, at having its entire world dismantled. A skittish sun was beginning to pierce through the mantle of fog. I should have been like that patch of sunlight, oblivious to whether young boys gazed at it or not, unconcerned that it might find itself severed from the world by the fog. I ran my hand over my cheek: The fuzz was thick. I would become a man with coarse hair on his face, and the veins that had previously been hidden would show. The patch of sunlight deepened in color, and the fog began to hasten past, unraveling as if it were smoke from an unseen fire.

A flock of black ducks with dark blue patches on their fore-heads waddled into the water and hurriedly came out again. Two of them, the ones closest to me, took flight. Soon the entire flock fol-lowed. The lake was slowly emerging from the shadows. Kneeling on the rock, I scooped a few handfuls of water, washed my face, and drank. When the ripples had scattered and faded, the water became a mirror. In it I saw reflected my head with cropped hair. That face, with no hair falling across the forehead, did not seem my own. For a long time I looked into those eyes, not because they were eyes, and my own, but because of everything they held within them, because of everything they had seen. My heart gave a start. The fear that had visited me the day before as I traversed the forest had returned. I closed my eyes to hide from myself. If I did not see my reflection, it meant that I was not there, that that fear was not there . . . Go home . . . I opened my eyes. In the water, beneath my face, I saw another face just like my own, with that same birth-mark on the forehead. The lips moved as though uttering words I could not hear. The eyes hardened. I leaned forward trying to make out the words . . . and the words that had eluded me and that I wanted to hear became intelligible . . . Go home. Everything will be lost if you do not go back . . . everything is still the same as you left it. Go back. The corner with the thatched roof to protect the camellias from the winter frost is the same; the reservoir filled with water for irrigation, with its flowering water plants swaying, the same; the spot at the end of the field, with the toolshed and the pile of neatly cut canes ready to be driven into the ground, to make trellises for the carnations that have not stopped flowering all sum-mer—carnations and buds, buds and carnations—is still the same; the rosebush with the yellow climbing roses that will soon reach

beyond the rooftop railing, the same; the good earth that is yours
. . . Come back! Come back! Your mother died calling your name
. . . Adrià . . . Adrià . . . come back . . . come back. Round pebbles,
egg-shaped pebbles, framed the face beneath my face, white, pink,
dark, in the shifting sand.

The water in the lake was turning blue. The face beneath my
face was slowly sinking, vanishing; only the eyes remained. A
sudden ray of the strongest sun whisked them away to who knows
what sands, who knows what roots . . . go back, go back, go back,
said the water . . . go back . . . go back.

XXXVIII

THE FISHERMAN

HEY, KID, COME OVER HERE AND HELP ME . . . A HUNDRED METERS away, a man was fishing. He was sitting on a folding stool. A satchel and a can full of worms lay at his side. I sat down next to him just as he leaned backward spinning a reel at the bottom of the rod, until out of the water sprang a small fish with the hook through its gills, wiggling furiously and flapping its tail against its mouth. He carefully removed it from the fishhook and returned it to the lake, just as Eva had said she did when she caught a fish that was too small. The fish became a faint shadow in the water. Hand me a worm. Careful not to squeeze it. He baited the fishhook and with a jerk of his arm cast the line as far as he could. What's your name? Adrià. Adrià what? Adrià Guinart. He laughed. Like the outlaw? I laughed too, not fully understanding what he meant, and when I was about to tell him that I was lost, he said in a low voice—Quiet! or the fish won't bite. I was distracted and didn't realize that he had caught a fish until he hurled it at me. Put it inside the satchel. It was slimy in my hands. It had a round, velvety tongue, slick, short. When he had caught half a dozen more, he stopped. He asked me to take the satchel, disassembled his rod, and headed behind some trees where he had parked a white car that seemed to be made of iron. Get in.

The house was wooden, surrounded by tall, old trees. Inside was a large room with a bed in one corner and, on the right, a hearth embedded in a stone wall. Three or four terra-cotta pots full of tobacco pipes sat on the mantelpiece. There were two doors at the end of the room, one leading to the kitchen, the other to the shower. Light the fire. Here, some newspapers. From the wad of folded newspapers I extracted one, and just as I was about to tear it up to make balls to place under the firewood, I encountered an entire page of photographs and, at the top, in the center, standing in front of a wall covered with half-torn posters, was Eva. She was laughing, but her eyes were sad. The fisherman came out of the kitchen, and I scrambled to hide the page with her picture. Hand me a sheet of the newspaper. I finished building the fire and when I was putting a match to it, the fisherman called me to come and help him. The fish kept slipping through his fingers and he couldn't cut them open. Grab it by the tail! Grab it with a dishrag! He placed them on a grill and cooked them over the fire. A cat that until then had not made its presence known brushed against my legs. It was dark grey, its eyes as blue as the fisherman's. I couldn't eat even one sad bite. The page with Eva's picture was folded and tucked in my pocket. The fisherman puffed on his pipe, the cat ate the fish scraps. Now, time for a nap. I always sleep after lunch. You, too. He walked me to the kitchen and, through a door next to the one that led outside, we entered a shed filled with tools, sacks of potatoes, all kinds of tins, and apples that were strewn across the floor. You'll sleep here, he said pointing to a workbench. Unclutter it. Wait, I'll give you a few pillows for a mattress. When I had the pallet set up, I lay down on the worktop. Eva laughed but her eyes were sad. I heard the fisherman stirring in the living room and I hid the picture. Not an hour had gone by when he called me. Let's go out, we'll gather the wood I cut a few days ago. It was a clear afternoon, not a cloud in sight, the sky a wilted blue, a mountain to my right. See that mountain? The sun rises on the other side. A mystery lies at the foot of it. Let's go.

—◅

We got in the car and headed for the mountain; it was quite high, parts of it covered with dark green trees, others studded with rocks. You see the pond at the foot? The car circled around and came to a stop. Get out. See that hole on the other side of the pond? Many years ago, a train was supposed to come through this part of the world, and the idea was to make a hole in the mountain to build a tunnel. The project started with great fanfare, but it didn't get very far. Everyone started dying: first, the engineer, then the fore-man, then another foreman. Then the workers . . . they all started dying, not in accidents but from illnesses. They kept bringing in new workers. Until three or four of them, the ones tasked with filling the barricades with gunpowder, just went under, sank. One of them managed to escape with his life and recounted, crossing himself many times, that the earth had given way, plunging deep, deep. Half the mountain, he said, had sunk, swallowing up men and trolleys. The work was halted and the mountain was left as it is today, with the gaping hole at the foot of it, large and wide, as black as an ugly wound. But the curious thing is that the earth in front of the opening slowly began to sink, and the great horseshoe-shaped hollow that hugs the entrance of the cave began to fill with water, the origin of which no one has ever been able to determine. It's a peculiar kind of water, thick and fetid green, sickening. No one has dared go in it and swim to the hole. If you throw a piece

of wood or a branch in it, it doesn't float, it eddies under. Watch
. . . we approached and stood two meters from the water; he picked
up a piece of wood and flung it as hard as he could; it landed in
the middle of the water and was immediately sucked under into a
great, green whirlpool. The locals wove a legend: Before the place
became a sinkhole, it had been a cave where a girl who was being
pursued had once sought refuge. On many nights, they said, she
could be heard singing. I have come here many an evening, at
different hours, and on all manner of nights—foggy, windy, hot,
gelid, moonlit—and I have never heard a girl singing. But legends
are beautiful and they help pass the time. Let's go. We headed to
the forest to collect the tree trunk and branches that had already
been chopped. We'll transport the wood at our leisure and tomorrow we'll stack it inside the shed. There should be enough for a
good two months.

We worked well into the night, first loading the wood and then
unloading it. At dinnertime again I could hardly swallow a thing.
An apple, and that was it. The cat wouldn't let me. It jumped on my
knees, crawled up my back, nibbled at my ears. What's the matter,
not feeling well? The fisherman sucked on his tobacco pipe and
stared me in the eye. He had sun-wizened skin, three deep wrinkles that creased his forehead from side to side, kind eyes. He wore
high, camel-colored boots, and what little shirt was visible under
his sweater appeared to be silk. As the cat dozed on my lap, he
started telling me about his life, though I didn't much care to hear
about it: He had two daughters whom he had not seen in years, he
liked them better from afar because it allowed him to see them as
he would have wished them to be. He had married young, and his
bride was beautiful. I never fell out of love. The daughters we had

are the spitting image of their mother. A year after our second was born, their mother died. All of my love—so much of it I hardly knew what to do with it—reverted to my daughters. I never took a step without their knowing. A rich man, I was able to provide everything they wanted and more. I strove to anticipate their every wish. They grew up, and I fell in love again. The girl was splendid, a springtime of joy, much younger than me. But the drama began when I introduced her to my daughters. They repudiated her. Our home became a battleground. And for them, I renounced what would have been my link to life. Until they were of an age to marry. You listening? They both married around the same time, to a couple of lowlifes who snatched them away from me. By that I mean they turned my daughters against me. They took them from their father. One day we were all together, and I don't recall what I was saying, but I lost my train of thought when I realized they weren't listening, so I stopped short. This happened on several occasions, until I realized they drew great satisfaction from seeing me lose my train of thought. His mind is deteriorating. I could almost hear them. I could just imagine them. And once his faculties become impaired, he will die, and we will be rich for the rest of our lives. I've always been one to give without waiting to be asked, and I wanted to put an end to that troubling situation, to that sordid state of affairs. Are you listening? I decided to sell everything I owned, properties, homes, farmhouses, arable lands, apartment buildings in the city . . . I converted it all to cash and divided it into four parts: one for my eldest daughter, one for my other daughter, a third for charity, and the fourth for me. And I have shut myself away here, with my forest, my moonlit skies, my rivers and my lakes . . . and with this cat that seems to have fallen in love with you. Off to bed now! If the lightbulb doesn't work (sometimes the filaments burn out), you'll find a candle and matches in the shed. Good night. The candle and the matches are on the first shelf of the medicine cabinet above the workbench.

XXXIX

THE FALL

ALTHOUGH THE LIGHT WORKED, I TOOK THE CANDLE AND MATCH-box and placed them on a crate next to the workbench. The cat had followed me and now sat by a heap of sawdust. My head was filled with thoughts, sullied by thoughts. It felt as though my brain had been turned inside out. I studied Eva's picture for a long time, then tucked it under the pillow, neatly folded. I usually liked the smell of apples, but that day it was making me dizzy, and I cracked the door to let the smell escape. I stretched out on the bench with the light off. The pillows were soft, but I had the same problem I had encountered when I was napping: If I moved, the pillows separated. I was forced to lie as still as a corpse. I dozed off and then woke again. I couldn't fall into a sound sleep. I had visions of the hearth, the red-winged flames curling up the chimney, licking the blackened bricks, the logs changing shapes, with the grill above them, and on the grill, smoking and weeping as they emptied themselves of lake water, the fish, all neatly lined up. I stretched out my arm and, grasping the box of matches, I sat up on the makeshift bed with my legs dangling. The flame from the first match rose high above the tiny stick and then inched down-ward in fits and starts, trembling, growing shorter, as the slender piece of wood turned black and started to coil, assuming the shape of a ringlet. I lit ten matches, and as the flame fluttered—white at the bottom, orange at the top—it occurred to me that one tiny flame such as that would suffice to set fire to an entire forest. The air would fan the flames, allowing them to spread their wings, lighting new flames, turning the whole forest into a resin-tinged scream which, after every speck of life had been set ablaze, would come to rest as quiet embers. But it was not the match or the flame that was foremost in my mind, it was Eva. The cat was no longer by the sawdust. A bird was pecking on wood. Pecking and pecking. The smell of apples escaped out the door and in poured the starlight and the scent of night. A beak was pecking on a piece of wood. Pecking and pecking. A beak pecked on a piece of wood . . . I climbed down from the workbench and tripped on the crate. The night was glassy, littered with dead stars; the moon was high, bluer than the icy snow of the celestial cemetery. The grass was damp. The mountain—a black silhouette against the black gleam of night—beckoned. I started toward it down a path so smooth and even that I could not hear my own footsteps. I stopped by the pond to listen: The voice, coming from afar as though rising from the depths of the water, was so sweet that it made me want to drop to my knees. Who was I? I had no bones, no nerves, no will. The song was lulling me to sleep, quelling every thought. A beak was pecking on wood. Pecking and pecking. Standing by the shore, I looked into the water and saw the stars yearning to flee their own death and leap to some unknown part in their urge to streak the vault of the sky with tangled moonthreads, shrieking, frenzied. I knelt and was searching for a twig to toss into the water, when suddenly someone shoved me into the pond, and I was swallowed up like an olive. I coursed through the whirlpool as if I were in a gurgling sink that was being emptied, swallowing everything it could. I was spinning as I was being sucked under; I felt a drunken sort of dizziness, and yet I still had my senses about me. Then the downward spin seemed to stop and the water, rather than pull me down, was pushing me forward. I was dying. I opened and closed my hands as I tried to cling to something, but I found only slimy water that reeked of blood. A beak was pecking on wood. When I thought that everything had come to an end, my feet lodged somewhere and I found myself lying on a beach rocked by silent waves. I could not feel a thing, but I knew I had to rise, I could not lie there forever; if I wanted to save myself, I had to keep going. Someone seized me by the nape like a cat and set me down on my feet with the water up to my belly. I swayed a little to avoid losing my balance. It was as if I had just been born, I hardly knew how to walk. One step after the other . . . one step after the other . . . A tenuous voice embraced me. I found myself sinking only to rise again . . . The water came up to my chest now. I finally reached a lacerated stone wall: I was edging closer to the song. The roof of the cave sang, the water sang. The song came from below, from above, from everywhere. I was enveloped by a cobweb voice that was like a thread spun by the Virgin Mary, showing me the path to follow. I stretched out an arm and felt a stone ridge. And in that instant there was a great commotion, as though a glass mountain had crumbled nearby. I glimpsed a distant light and that light drew me toward it. I felt, time and again, that it was almost at hand, and yet it stayed forever beyond my reach. I wanted to scream but could not, I wanted to run but could not. And then my nose caught, stronger than ever, the familiar scent of yellow roses, the kind that do not smell like red roses, but have the simple fragrance of dawn-fresh roses that have bloomed with great effort, earning their scent by their patience and finally able to share it: the scent from the rosebush at home that climbed all the way to the rooftop. The song, the rose . . . none of it was real! Not the murmur of the water cascading down a horsetail-shaped waterfall, not the sharp ridges of the crumbling rock wall. But the light was drawing nearer, I was almost to it . . . deep in the entrails of the earth, lost, never to find my way out. The walls gleamed, the rocks going up and the rocks going down gleamed. A moonbeam filtered through a crack near the ceiling and spilled onto a slab, upon which lay a girl. The most dream-like dream of all dreams! I approached the slab. The girl—I could see her clearly—naked as a lily, with violet eyes dappled with specks of gold, was Eva. Lying on the stone that was her bed, neither seeing nor breathing, she seemed to be made of ice. A hand of the palest white fell limply from the stone slab. I wanted to hold it, but as I tried to move closer I found that my feet were tied, and the more I strained, the tighter my ankles were griped by whatever it was that bound me. Until I jerked so furiously that everything shook and glass powder rained down on me. Someone was laughing at me. Someone I could not see was playing with my feelings, with my life, so that I would know that it was not my life, but had simply been loaned to me and was at that person's disposal. If ever a boy had yearned to love a girl, that boy was I. To hold her hand in mine . . . but I could not reach it . . . A beast leapt from the ceiling and fell upon me. I lay half dead. When I came to, the shaft of moonlight fell far from the stone. I was holding a handful of bones—bones that had once been a hand. I released my grip, fearing they might break into tiny bits, and I heard myself muttering, poor bones, poor bones, as though trying to appease them, lest they attacked me. I had become deranged. I wished I were not me, I wished I were above rather than below, a tree hugging the earth, deeply rooted, with branches aloft, the sun overhead, blue skies overhead, the furious aliveness of the stars overhead. Snow rain frost. For the birds not to nest in my branches but to come and sing in them. My tresses of leaves tousled by the winds . . . Who was licking my face? Someone was running a tongue over my cheek, again and again. I found it difficult to open my eyes. The cat's face was next to mine. I was lying at the entrance to the toolshed, half in, half out, my feet caught in a rope that led to a tangled pile of ropes by one of the legs of the workbench.

XL

LATER

WHAT ARE YOU DOING ON THE FLOOR? THE FISHERMAN WAS
standing at the kitchen door looking at me. The cat had jumped
on top of me. Come have some breakfast and then we'll tidy up
this mess . . . What on earth? You need to disentangle your leg
from that rope. I understood without fully understanding. The
workbench was no longer against the wall; the medicine cabinet,
its doors wide open, was bare. The empty bottles that I recalled
seeing neatly lined up in rows by the door were now scattered
about. The pillows that had been on the bench lay on the floor. It
could not be. I had not dreamed that I slipped out during the night
and a bird was pecking and pecking on a tree as I headed to the
pond. I had lived all of that. I did not dream that the moon was
blue, the grass damp . . . The bottoms of my trousers had been wet.
They were now dry, but I had felt them sodden against my legs. I
had seen the sky reflected in the water . . . and I still held in my
hand . . . what was I holding in my hand? Nothing. It was empty.
And what had those stones and the shower of broken glass been?
And the fall? Had the real and the imagined merged so that I was
no longer able to discern what was true and what a product of my
dreams?

The fire was lit, the pitcher of milk was steaming, the entire
room smelled of coffee. The honey in the pot—flower juice in
a glass prison, the fisherman called it—awaited a spoon, and,

skewered with an iron prong, two slices of bread were toasting. The cut I had on my right thumb throbbed. I ate nothing. Did you wrestle with a wolf last night? Don't tell me your dream if you don't want to, but I'd like to hear it. I'd like to know why you fell off the bench, and most of all why you slept on the floor, and why you didn't get up from there. Go on, tell me. I never dream, I lied.

We worked the whole day without pause, tidying up the tool-shed and bringing in the wood from the forest. Why don't you stay? I shrugged my shoulders. You've seen for yourself that it's comfortable enough around here. I could fix up the shed for you and build another one to house all these oddments. You seem lost and I sense you could use a guiding hand. You're very young. I was inclined to tell him that I enjoyed nothing more than wandering through the world lost. Doing as I pleased no matter how things turned out, with no one giving me any advice. Seeing the sky, the forests, experiencing fear, contemplating the night and having it for a roof.

Toward evening, sitting in front of the house, a strawberry and saffron sunset before us, he again asked me to stay. I like you. It would please me if you would be my son. I like you because you sometimes appear older than your age and at other times you seem like a child. When I didn't respond, he asked me to tell him about my life. Won't you? I took a while to reply, my whole being enthralled by the saffron and strawberry hues. I did not want to say anything that did not come from my very core. I closed my eyes for a moment to disentangle myself from the twilight sky; I had to think before speaking. My life is my own, I began, placing my hand on my chest. A few months ago, I don't know how many, I still had a pocket knife with a fork, spoon, corkscrew, and screwdriver that my father had given me, but I gave it away. And now the only thing I have is my own life. If I speak about it, it escapes, I lose it. He gave me a pat on the back, almost laughing as he did so. I know, I added, that all lives are more or less the same in the essentials. He thrust his head back and closed his eyes, leaving just a slit open to spy on whatever it was he wanted to see. Don't make me laugh. What will you do, restlessly drifting from place to place? Do you want to end up sleeping on the street or in a church portico when you are an old man? I don't care. I want to roam the world. Be from everywhere and nowhere. I've only just begun to see things, and it makes my head spin to think of what there is still to be seen. So many towns, so many paths . . . He again patted me on the back. And, if in the end you have seen all the villages in the world, what then? Like the lives you spoke of, they too are more or less the same: with straight or winding streets and houses piled one on top of the other. What is important, I responded, is the eye we cast on these villages. Yes, of course, and the same goes for how we look at people, but the moment will come when you will have a false life on your hands. You, what do you have inside? A garden or an inferno? A bit of both. It depends on how the wind blows. And, without knowing exactly why, I asked him: What does it mean to be like Cain? Until then he had spoken without looking at me, but the question made him turn his head. What do you mean? Just that: What does being like Cain mean? Do you mean to tell me that you don't know the story? I know God first punished him and then protected him. When I made my mother cross she would say I reminded her of Cain. And this mark here on my forehead . . . What a question to ask. Everyone knows that Cain killed . . . but some people regard him as someone who seeks knowledge, who never relents, who lets nothing stop him, who wants to know everything there is to be known. What a question to ask, he added, shaking his head. I left home so that I could encounter new villages, meet people, and because I was tired of my mother . . . and nothing could have stopped me. And also so I could go off to war. Although I've had the war close-at-hand, I can't say I have experienced it, because I fled from it as often as I could. The fisherman rose. Well, I'm afraid you're late. You better hurry if you still want to find it. Let's have dinner. I followed him. He turned around before entering the house. Oh, and whenever you want to go, just go. Don't say anything. I don't like goodbyes. You'll find everything you need—clothes and food—in the shed.

XLI

THE RIVER

I WALKED FOR A LONG TIME. I TRAIPSED FROM ONE VILLAGE TO
the next, from one path to another. Every road was deserted, every
house destroyed. Early one morning I tripped over a dead dog;
it had a piece of cardboard around its neck with some words that
had been smudged by the rain: "Follow this dog. He will lead you
to me. I'm wounded." Occasionally, I would encounter men coming toward me, emaciated, with famished faces, holding each other
up, their feet and legs wrapped in rags bound with rope, and I
would take a different route. On one occasion, an aircraft flew by
overhead three or four times, so low that the pilot must have seen
me even though I ducked. But I wasn't worth a bullet, much less a
bomb. A bell tower in what was left of a village gave me shelter.
That arrow that surged skyward accompanied me for a while, and
after leaving it behind I turned around to look at it. A clutch of
deranged creatures leapt out of the bushes, brandishing guns, and
fled in the direction of a hill shouting "Kill 'em! Kill 'em all!" Until
I found myself standing by a wide river I had never seen before,
its banks bombed and strewn with bodies, as though the dead had
been assembled there and piled on top of each other, ready to be
moved somewhere else. Dead men who seemed to be asleep, on
their sides, their legs drawn up; dead men with eyes open to the
sky, dead men without legs, without arms . . . skeletons of soldiers
with bones picked clean by the birds. And, scattered among the

dead, charred upturned trucks, destroyed machinery, tanks with the dead driver still inside the gun turret. A burned hand with curled fingers next to a rifle. Tents—and bits of tarpaulin from tents—being winnowed this way and that by the wind. Bombed bridges swept downstream by the river, pieces of wood still gripping the shore, ravaged fields of thyme. In a trench (there were so many of them, deep, like the tracks of giant snakes), three dogs scurried away on hearing me, their tails low, but a skinny, grungy one stood its ground. And above so much death, the flight of large birds with long, featherless necks. A line of crows were preening their wings and chests on an airplane wing that was lodged in the ground, surrounded by rowboats and charred wood. I raised an arm to drive them away. Some lazily took flight, but three remained, perched on the half-buried airplane that rested between the bank and the shallows of that smooth-flowing river, whose course was only occasionally disturbed by wooden planks from bridges. And, pervading everything, the stench of death.

They will bury them soon; they come in their trucks every two or three days. At first they had to flee because they were being shot at. Not anymore . . . I turned around when I heard that voice. What a relief to see someone alive, a young woman, though haggard, her eyes still moist. She was holding a dead baby in her arms; I could tell immediately that it was dead by the waxen color of the legs and the hand that hung limply. She spoke to the child as if it were alive, my love, my baby . . . With a strange look on her face, she stared directly into the eyes of a dead man lying by the edge of the water—not far enough in for the current to carry him away—as if the poor man, with his crushed head and chest, were to blame for the war. They dump them in mass graves farther up, sometimes they burn them, but not always. They can't handle all the bodies, they're overwhelmed. And meanwhile the vultures are getting fatter. Thank God the war is over. I witnessed the end of it; it ended right here in this river, and the river carried it out to sea. My house was up there. Only the four walls are still standing. We had a vegetable garden that was glorious . . . just think about it, with the river right here to draw water from. I sleep a long way from here now, but I come every now and then to see if I can find a soldier who's still breathing and can tell me where my husband died . . . Everyone says I shouldn't expect him to return . . . I listen, without saying anything, but I don't believe he's dead. Did you fight in the war, too? You have the dry skin that comes with starvation, and your eyes seem to be set deep in a cave, but your sunken eyes wouldn't matter if it weren't for the fact that they're filled with apprehension, no, that's not it . . . with horror . . . If you knew the screams I have heard, screams of wounded men crying out for help, sobbing and shouting their unspeakable grief . . . and then suddenly I would spot a hand rising in search of some kind of mercy, only to drop to the ground again because it was all over. Come with me . . . you're so young, I wish I could help you . . . My husband's name was Pere; he was taller than me and had black eyes, same as his hair . . . perhaps you met him . . . She looked me straight in the eyes and I felt an unbearable rush of shame. Shame at having run away from the war the way some flee the plague, alone, always alone with myself; shame at not having defended something, without knowing exactly what that thing was, which I should have defended as countless others had . . . all of me imprisoned inside my own sad skin, withered from hunger, just as the woman with the dead baby with his head against her breast had said. She straightened the child and turned him to face me; his eyes were open, his mouth tightly closed . . . I helped them fill sacks with earth; all the women in the village, not far from here, filled sacks with earth. We needed more hands. If you had heard the cannons and machine guns going off, if you had seen the airplanes dropping rosary upon rosary of bombs. If you had seen the light of the burning fires in the dead of night . . . an inferno lasting months and months. Years and years . . . years will have to pass before anything can be sowed by the river, because when they start digging they'll find bones, not earth. The only thing left: bones. The bones of the nameless dead. That mountain range—see it?—the top was blown off by the shrapnel that pounded it repeatedly, in a never-ending punishment. I still don't know how my son and I survived, but the terror he experienced has left him unable to shut his eyes, not even to sleep. We should be dead, he and I, and you wouldn't have found anyone to tell you all this . . . She fell silent, facing the river that flowed wide, her eyes fixed on the turbid waters that seemed to soothe her and carry her thoughts downstream. She left a while later, without glancing at me, without a word.

XLII

IRE

AN OLD, DILAPIDATED BOAT, PAINTED AND REPAINTED, RESTED against the wing of the airplane. The river was placid and the afternoon subdued, a lone afternoon in the middle of the world, animated only by the flight of birds that soared and soared before swooping down on the dead. The other riverbank was the same as the one I had just left behind, with its dead devoured by carrion birds. I pushed the boat far onto the bank so it wouldn't be washed away. At dusk I came to the edge of a forest. I was again overtaken by the smell of trees; it was a relief to have branches and leaves for a roof. I started down a path that entered the woods amid tall grasses. From afar, I glimpsed a window with a light on inside. It was a deceptive light: When you thought you had almost reached it, it was still far away. I walked for a long time before I arrived at the clearing where a half-brick, half-wooden shack stood next to a well. The light from the window fell in front of the well. Beside it something gleamed. Before peeking through the window to see who lived in that shack in the woods, I leaned down . . . I picked up the object and could hardly believe it: In my hand I held a knife just like the one I had given Eva the day I met her so she wouldn't forget me, the one that was good for so many things. The screw-driver was missing the tip. Who could she have given it to, or who could have taken it from her, and how had it reached that corner of the woods? Had the person who had taken it from her lost it while drawing water from the well? Or on the day after a battle? I was so preoccupied with the knife in my hand that it wasn't until a good while later that I walked over to the window and peered inside the house.

At the far end of the room hung a yellow-and-blue flowered curtain, and in front of it sat an old woman with a dark scarf around her head, a black shawl draped over her shoulders, and large eyeglasses. Her hand rose and fell rhythmically, pulling a thread. On one side of the curtain was an armoire with two doors, and on top of it a green jug and a bottle holding a candle. The old woman rose and approached the window. I quickly ducked. I circled the house on all fours. At the back of the house, by a window with closed shutters, stood the tallest, broadest tree I had ever seen. The fluttering of birds could be heard coming from deep within the branches. Firewood was stacked next to a cage, blocking my way, and beyond it was a henhouse. I couldn't spot any windows on the wall where the flowered curtain hung on the inside of the shack, but I did see a pile of wood reaching almost to the roof, covering the entire wall. That, and a few bundles of heather. Just as I turned the corner and was about to walk by the entrance, the door swung open and a voice shouted: Who's out there? The old woman emerged from the house with an axe in her hand, a dark silhouette against the light inside, tiny and rotund, her voice powerful. Why don't you answer? What are you staring at? Answer me! If you heard she was beautiful, you're a bit late! Three weeks late. I moved closer. When she saw me clearly in the light of the house, she lowered the axe. What are you doing here? Answer me!

I said I was crossing the forest and was thirsty; the water in the river was disgusting, but I hadn't dared draw water from the well for fear that the pulley would creak and betray my presence. Why didn't you want to be discovered? I blurted out the first thing that came to mind: To avoid frightening the people who might be inside the house. She burst out laughing, tossing her head back. Come in, she ordered when she finally stopped laughing. You got money on you? No, I said. Come in! I don't want it to be said that I haven't been charitable at least once in my lifetime. Who told you there was a house so deep in the forest? I wanted to say that my feet had led me there but I was wary of angering her. I followed the path, I was fleeing from the river . . . the axe gleamed, it looked sharp.

Inside it reeked of smoke and boiled cabbage. A fire was blazing in the small hearth; a box beside the chair where I had seen the old woman sitting held balls of yarn of different colors. Hanging above the hood over the hearth was a painting in a black frame, the glass more dirty than clean and, inside it, an embroidered Virgin Mary: the same that graced my religious medallions. I put my hand in the back pocket of my trousers: They weren't there. I checked my neck: I wasn't wearing them. Then I took a good look at the old woman; she was ugly as the devil, with a short, flat nose, small, wide-set eyes, a low forehead, puffy cheeks, and a large mouth. She removed some knickknacks from a round table, and once the table had been cleared she brought out a bottle and two glasses. You'll see how pleasant this will be . . . sit here, I'll sit facing you. Speak! I glanced at the fireplace hood and then at her; I couldn't help but compare the embroidered face with the real one. She guessed what I was thinking and started to laugh in that manner of hers, with her head tilted back, the skin of her neck taut and her Adam's apple trembling. You're seeing visions. Take a good look at me. Are you

mute, or did the cat get your tongue? I'm telling you, you're seeing visions. She was better at lying than the most deceitful of liars.
The Virgin Mary was her, just like that man had said. The Virgin
Mary on my religions medallions, all the faces of every Virgin
Mary, were her face. She must have really loved herself. Ugly as
sin, she loved herself. How could she love herself, so fat and ugly?
. . . I certainly couldn't imagine embroidering my own face, with
so many faces to choose from in this world. When I was a little girl
the nuns taught me to embroider. You can't imagine how often I
have blessed them. But don't think embroidery is my only talent.
She rose and drew back the flowered curtain; behind it was a cot
covered with a red bedspread and an armchair with ropes attached
to the armrests and the legs. Newish ropes, still white, not very
thick. She brought an ashtray and placed it on the table, sat down,
and lit a cigarette. You smoke? I shook my head. Well, I do. The
soldiers got me in the habit. They always bring me some. Smoke,
old woman, smoke . . . that'll keep you entertained . . . and in my
old age, I smoke and admire the smoke coming out of my mouth
and the smoke I expel through my nostrils. Leaning forward, she
held the cigarette up to my face, you got to ginger up. How can
you go around with those helpless-creature eyes of yours? Aren't
you a man? Lift up your heart then! And hurrah for war and death!
She left the cigarette in the ashtray, uncorked the bottle, and filled
the glasses to the top. This will loosen up your tongue, liven up
your blood. Drink up! She lifted her glass, I lifted mine and emptied it in one swallow, as she did. To the religious medallions! The
wine was like fire. I like you, even if you've gone mute. I suppose
you could be given communion without having to confess. I wasn't
expecting to have such good company tonight. Throw a log on the
fire. Drink! Peaceful night, it is . . . the rumblings of war reached

this far, in case you're wondering. I admit I don't know the meaning of the word fear. Never did! She eyed her cigarette and I the ropes on the armchair. Look at me! You've never seen anyone like me. Never, never! She filled her glass again. Drink up! And she filled mine again, too. That armchair, she said, stretching out her arm with the glass in her hand, has quite a story. The girl who used to sit in it is buried by the tree in the back, under the rabbit cage. The oldest tree of them all. It was full of birds and she liked looking at it. I turned the armchair around so she couldn't see it. I covered up the window: shutters closed and a pile of wood over them. So she couldn't see a thing. Some of them birds have white and black feathers, some have red chests—red from eating so many cherries—some have plumage as green as stagnant water, others grey with blue bellies, all of them chirping and flitting about, and she with her back to them so she'd see only me. Me! I had her for a long time. She was beautiful. There's no explaining how beautiful she was. When they took me to her . . . she was unconscious by the vegetable garden, next to the cabbage patch. A bullet had perforated her thigh. Not gone through it, mind you, it was lodged inside. And with the kitchen knife . . . No, with a knife she had in her pocket, which had some other tools that were just a nuisance, I dug out the bullet . . . and with these two fingers. The wound got infected. Every day I had to squeeze out the pus and dress it with rags soaked in thyme water. As I nursed her I kept thinking she was mine . . . Drink up! She poured me more wine, too much, and it spilled over. Drink up! I'm pouring you wine so you'll drink it, not so you'll let it go bad. It burned. It burned my throat. After I'd nursed her back to health I decided to keep her forever. Those cords you've been looking at were for tying her up; otherwise she would have escaped. Tied up. Nice and tight, to keep the old woman in the woods company. Drink! Don't you think she'd have run away if she could, scampering into the forest like a hare? She'd have flown out the window if she'd had wings . . . The first to have her was a middle-aged man who was running away from the bullets and was hungry for . . . I stepped outside so he wouldn't feel self-conscious and I heard her scream. How crude of her. And then, what a cry! What a cry the little bird let out. It must have reached the depths of hell. When the man came out he thanked me. I didn't hold out my hand, but he slipped some coins into my pocket. Thank you. And after that first one, others started coming. Sometimes they had to line up . . . had more lice than a hens' nest filled with old straw.

I couldn't breathe. What was her name? She downed another glass and dried her lips on her sleeve. A funny name. What would you guess it was? She had the same name as the mother of men. Funny, isn't it? I gulped down the wine that was left in the glass and choked. Stifling a laugh, huh? Like the mother of all men. Eva, Eva, Eva . . . I used to say to her: Eva, lucky day when I found you more dead than alive by the cabbage patch. What a stroke of luck! And she thought only of running away. I bound her tighter every day. Soon she had red marks, a girdle of raw flesh around her wrists and ankles. I had to put the food in her mouth; sometimes she'd swallow it, sometimes she'd spit it out. Until one night, when I had already closed the shutters and was bolting the door, seven men the color of chestnuts showed up, all of them the color of chestnuts, and I lent her to them for the night. Here, take her. They hauled her off into the woods; she was as still as death and didn't let out a cry. They took her away, holding her aloft like a goat . . . all the while I had her here she never shed a tear. She struggled to get loose, and the harder she struggled the deeper the ropes cut into her skin . . . but I never saw her cry. I would have liked to see a tear, at least one, in those eyes the color of violets. But no. Never. She didn't come back. They didn't bring her back. I found her the following morning at daybreak, naked under the trees, with a branch stuck up her, thrust where life is born. She drank again and clicked her tongue. She went to fetch another bottle. Fixing her eyes on me as she uncorked it, she filled her glass and, without taking her eyes off me, filled mine and then emptied her own with one gulp. Drink! With violet eyes . . . you'll sleep outside. You're young, the night won't do you no harm. I'll lend you a blanket. No, two: one to place under you, the other on top. You'll see how pleasant it is to sleep under the trees. Tomorrow, in exchange for food, you will help me clean the rabbit cage.

I jumped up, nearly out of my mind, grabbed a log from the fireplace and, without stopping to think what I was doing, I struck her. She was left with one eye open. I don't know where I got the strength, but I dragged her to the armchair, sat her in it, and bound her wrists and ankles to the legs and armrests. I walked outside with a burning log, panting, my eyes bulging, and went around to the back of the house, to the pile of wood by the wall. Tongues of fire immediately rose from the bundles of heather, everything crackled. The shack quickly turned into a furnace, and the nearest leaves and branches screamed as they caught fire. Clutching Eva's penknife in one hand and the burning log in the other, I went about wildly setting fire to all the grasses, the bushes, the low-lying branches.

I stopped at the edge of the forest, my hands and feet frozen, all of me a feverish knot, and hurled the burning log into the woods.

At first I couldn't find the rowboat, but when I finally stumbled upon it, I let myself fall inside. I felt like the boat was sinking and I was rising, that nothing separated me from the boat, that the river was standing up. I still don't know how I managed to drag it to the water, but somehow I found myself floating on the river with the oars in my hands. I rowed mechanically, lost in that nightmare, beneath a sky of hastening clouds, without knowing what to do, whether to let the current carry me downstream or to forge ahead . . . if, in the end, one shore was the same as the next and nothing made any difference. Only the river and myself. No war. No evil. I grasped Eva's knife, held it under the water, and then slowly opened my hand. The boat floated along on its own . . . until, with some effort, I reached the shore. A gleam of moonlight fell on me like a sword and was mirrored by the river. The fog—a low, sulphurous-yellow fog—was spreading, slowly shrouding the dead.

XLIII

Night's End

I'VE LOOKED FOR YOU. I'VE BEEN SEARCHING FOR YOU SINCE YESterday. As soon as you left I started looking. Where were you? I knew you would come back. The baby died, my son died. I was looking for you so you would help me bury him. The woman with the dead baby was carrying a lantern, which she handed to me. I was able to close his eyes. He doesn't look, he doesn't see, so beautiful . . . the child was wearing a lace-trimmed garment, like a Christening gown, with a white ribbon just below his chest. A lace bonnet tied with a silk ribbon framed his face. Look how beautiful. The woman with the dead baby had a shovel at her feet. Pick it up. We'll bury him farther down, where the ground is not so thick with the dead, in a hole made by a howitzer. The earth isn't as hard there because it's been turned. Close to the river, so it will lull him to sleep if he hears it. The woman's face was as pale as the child's: two faces as white as a sheet of paper against the sulphurous fog. I put the shovel inside the boat. You row, I don't know how to. The boat glided along the water, cutting through the wisps of fog that drifted by, though the evening was airless. Last night I realized that my son had died and I started looking for you. He'd be alive if he had been able to eat, but the food is all gone. A neighbor gave me this gown—see?—and with tears in her eyes she said, bury him all beautiful . . . She took my hand, your hand is as icy as my son's. Only the whisper of the oars and the water could be heard.

This is it. I recognize it from the flag, from the flagpole planted in the ground that the flash of moonlight just illuminated. I took the lantern and the shovel and helped her out of the boat, her child still in her arms. Can you feel how the earth slopes a bit under your feet?

The turned earth was soft in places, hard in others. Dig deep. She kept saying. Dig deeper. If you don't make it deep enough the dogs will get to him and the birds will gouge his eyes out. If you tire, take a break, we have the whole night. Deeper. As deep as you are tall. I don't want the dogs to find him . . . she grabbed me by the arm and squeezed it tightly. You hear that? Don't you hear a dog howling? They howl with their heads up and necks taut. They howl so they will be heard in the heavens, to frighten death away. Hurry, hurry . . . she tugged at my hair and laughed . . . she pinched my earlobe . . . Here, leave the shovel, take him. She handed me the baby. With the child in my arms I didn't dare breathe. She jumped into the hole to measure it. Drops of sweat blinded me, rolling down my cheeks, down my back. Ice cold. That's enough. I set the baby on the ground and helped her climb out of the hole. She gave me a shove. You shouldn't have put him down. I could have got out on my own. Enough, she said. Are you listening? Enough. Here, she handed me the baby. Don't drop him. Lay him face up, arrange his legs, adjust the ribbons, smooth out his gown. Put the shovel over his face with the blade down and the handle toward his feet, to protect it, to keep the earth out of his eyes. Wait a moment, don't start throwing earth on him. I heard her praying in a low voice nearly muffled by the water that was flowing near the child's final bed. Get out. Help me cover him with earth. Kneeling on either side of the hole, we started pushing earth inside with our hands, kicking earth on the ribbons, on the lace, on what had been her son. Stamp on it. Make it hard. We should mark it with a stone, so I will always know where he rests. I found one not far away, large and white. I wedged it into the earth and we both stood there for a moment looking at it. Let's go. It's done. I will come every day, at nightfall, at daybreak . . . We climbed into the rowboat. The mother of the dead baby sat facing me, holding the lantern. Suddenly she stood up, the boat tilted to the side, and she dropped the lantern. She pointed in front of her, her arm outstretched. I asked her what she had seen. Without replying, she sat down again. Don't you see the airplane wing? We're here. When the spring arrives . . .

I heard them before I saw them: a dull murmur upon the earth. Little by little they began to rise, dark and still. A breeze tousled their hair. They rose from the mass graves, from the middle of the river, gliding over the water as they crossed to the other shore. They dragged their feet, unfaltering, tall, blind. They were headed for the bombed mountain. Thousands of them. Suddenly a cloud was rent and, against the glassy sky, in front of that breach, a dark figure with arms extended began to take shape. Standing beside the figure was the angel from Mass, with folded wings, and he began to form the blue and crimson squares that would become the floor of the church, while the battalions of the dead grew in number as they marched toward the mountain. I climbed out of the boat followed by the mother of the dead baby. What do you see? I asked her. Do you see something? No. We stood in silence for a moment. Don't you hear the treading of countless feet? No. Can't you see an angel laying the floor of the church with dark blue and crimson squares, extending it toward us? He colors the squares slowly, as though from within. Some take longer to pigment. The squares on one side of the church absorb color faster and more intensely than the ones on the other side, they color so deeply it hurts your eyes. Now he's resting. He is spreading his wings, can't you see the shadows they cast? He is starting to blow the bubble that will become the Church of this world . . . he is blowing it up, broadening it, so it will shelter the dead, so they can be buried beneath its glass dome, which is so fine that a wisp of air could blow it away, a drop of rain would suffice to pierce it. Look, now he's forming the petals, and the petals will come together at the top of the bubble, and then . . . a lightless sun, transparent and golden in the dead of night, was slowly rising before the shadowy figure, and the shadowy figure accompanied it with its arms, as though ushering it toward the sky. Look . . . the angel is starting on the bell tower. Can you hear it? Don't you hear the breathing? I hear breathing, yes, it is the river's breath. Nothing more. The breath of the river and of the night. No, I said, it is the breath of the angel, and of the dead. And more are on their way. A river of angels has traversed the sky; they are descending fast. They are the helpers. They move from place to place pulling the petals up, up, to harden the bubble's shell. They are pushing the bell tower toward the sky, fast, fast. Don't you see them? My eyes are open and I see only the passing clouds embroidered with moonlight. Can't you see the smaller angels, each with one black wing and one white wing? They are making a crown. Listen! In this temple, built by the angels, built upon the faith of those who are coming toward me, I will fill the calix of my hand with dew and bless this night's sun, which is Jesus Christ the Innocent, giver of all things. From atop this ancient mountain, with no church, with no wooden altar, beyond the seas, beyond the rivers, from this summit with its crest of clouds and foundations of fog, I will bless the murderers and the murdered, the decaying flesh, the bones that fall apart, the veins that have flooded the earth with blood. I will bless the throngs of approaching souls, attracted by my piety, searching for my forgiveness. And the shadowy figure held out his arms and from the tips of his fingers issued lightning-colored filaments that descended upon the dead on both sides of the river, bringing them repose . . . and a white horse splattered with blood . . . and . . .

A blinding light coursing above the fog forced me to close my eyes. When I opened them, everything had faded: There were no angels, no shadows of marching soldiers. The mother of the dead baby turned around to face me, it's the trucks with the men who are coming to burn the dead, goodbye, she said, briefly touching my arm. *Adéu.*

It was difficult to set out again: I was leaving behind, inside the burning forest, so much charred life. I would return home to tend the carnation field, with the water flowing through the ditches, the sound of trains passing in the night, the rosebush with its yellow roses climbing to the rooftop. A different me would return. I had seen death up close. And evil. A great sadness like an iron hand clutched my heart. Where was home? Did I still have a home? I would return bearing mountains of memories of all the people I had met, people who had been born and had lived so that I might know them, and they would accompany me for the rest of my journey . . . so many sweet eyes, so many sad eyes, so many surprised eyes, so many desperate eyes . . . Would the remembrance of evil dissipate or would I carry it with me always, like a malady of the soul? The road was wide, I would have to find the path home. I did not know where it was. I felt as ancient as the world. I pondered everything that I had just seen but did not exist. No angels, no dead men drawing nearer, searching for peace at night's end. Only me and that fever. As the sun began its ascent in the sky, as every day, as always . . .

M ercè Rodoreda (1908–1983) is widely regarded as the most important Catalan writer of the twentieth century. Exiled in France and
Switzerland following the Spanish Civil War, Rodoreda began writing
the novels and short stories—*Twenty-Two Short Stories*, *The Times of the
Doves*, *Camellia Street*, *Garden by the Sea*—that would eventually make
her internationally famous, while at the same time earning a living as a
seamstress. In the mid-1960s she returned to Catalonia, where she continued to write. *Death in Spring* and *The Selected Stories of Mercè Rodoreda*
are also available from Open Letter.

M aruxa Relaño is a journalist and English-language translator working from Spanish and Catalan. She was a translator for the *Wall Street Journal* and wrote for the *New York Daily News*, *New York Sun*, *New York Magazine*, *Newsday*, and *Hoy Newspaper*, among others. Her recent co-translations include the novels *A Man of His Word* by Imma Monsó and *The Sea* by Blai Bonet.

M artha Tennent is an English-language translator who works primarily from Catalan and Spanish. She was born in the United States, but has lived most of her life in Barcelona. She received a fellowship from the National Endowment for the Arts for her translation of *The Selected Stories of Mercè Rodoreda*. Her work has appeared in *Epiphany*, *Two Lines*, *Words Without Borders*, *A Public Space*, *World Literature Today*, *PEN America*, and *Review of Contemporary Fiction*.

Open Letter—the University of Rochester's nonprofit, literary translation press—is one of only a handful of publishing houses dedicated to increasing access to world literature for English readers. Publishing ten titles in translation each year, Open Letter searches for works that are extraordinary and influential, works that we hope will become the classics of tomorrow.

Making world literature available in English is crucial to opening our cultural borders, and its availability plays a vital role in maintaining a healthy and vibrant book culture. Open Letter strives to cultivate an audience for these works by helping readers discover imaginative, stunning works of fiction and poetry, and by creating a constellation of international writing that is engaging, stimulating, and enduring.

Current and forthcoming titles from Open Letter include works from Argentina, Bulgaria, China, Iceland, Israel, Latvia, Poland, Spain, South Africa, and many other countries.